inhaler
Peds
underware

The Man They Called "Sudden Death"

Dropping the reins—already knotted for just such an emergency—Jim's hands came up holding guns. As they rose he fired both weapons and his attackers on the right and left went down. Then, with a pressure of his knees, he jumped the horse at the man in the middle. He cursed and tried to leap aside. He nearly succeeded, but the massive shoulder caught him and drove him into the dust.

THE OUTLAW TRAIL

BEN THOMPSON

LEISURE BOOKS • NEW YORK CITY

A LEISURE BOOK

Published by

Nordon Publications, Inc.
Two Park Avenue
New York, N.Y. 10016

one

Since his hurried departure from Fourways, Jim Green had not seen a human being, but had slept with his saddle for a pillow, and lived upon the game his gun had procured. His first thought now was for a square meal for himself and his mount.

About to enter the Buckhorn Saloon, that famous San Antonio rendezvous, the Texan paused abruptly, his eye caught by a single word on a square of paper affixed to the wall.

"Sudden!"

The crudely printed bill offered a reward of five hundred dollars for the apprehension of one "Sudden," wanted for robbery and murder. A description was given: "Young, dark hair and moustache, grey-blue eyes, dressed as a cowboy, wears two guns, and rides a black horse with a white blaze on face and white stockings on off foreleg." The notice bore the name of the sheriff of Fourways.

For a moment Jim stared at it in blank amazement, and then, as the full significance came home, anger surged within him. Not only was he to be hounded down for a crime of which he knew nothing, but he had been given a name which would follow him wherever he went. He was outlawed; the hand of every man would be against him, and he was liable to be shot like a mad dog. Impulsively, he raised a hand to tear away the placard.

"I wouldn't," a warning voice said. "If you want one as

a souvenir, there's others in less prominent places; the town is fair spotted with them. And if your horse tallies, that description would fit you pretty good," the stranger said.

Jim's jaw hardened. "If you had a black horse and mustache you might qualify your own self," he retorted.

"But I don't have neither of them things," the other grinned.

"Both of 'em can be got rid of," Jim pointed out. "See here, I'll match a dollar with you to settle which of us takes the other in and claims the cash."

The stranger laughed outright. "You're a cool card," he said. "No sir, they might glom on to the pair of us. I got a better proposition. I know a fella who'd be glad to meet you."

"If he's wearin' a star . . . "

"He ain't, and he's got no use for them as do," the unknown replied. "Hook up with him and you needn't let that—" he spat contemptuously at the notice—"scare you."

"Did I mention I was scared?"

The man nodded. "Ever hear of Rogue's Riders?" he asked.

Jim had. Under the leadership of a man named Roger, but more generally known as "Rogue," they were perhaps the most notorious of the bands of desperadoes who raided and robbed over a wide area of southwest Texas.

"Much obliged, but I figure I can take care of myself.

"Well, she's a free country. If you should find yourself crowded, head west till you come to the Split Rock—you can't mistake her—follow the left trail and you'll be looked after."

Jim nodded his thanks and turned away in the direction of the livery stable. Though he had displayed indifference to the man who had warned him, he had no illusions regarding the danger of his position and knew that he must get away from San Antonio as fast as possible. At any moment he could be linked up with that damn wanted poster. The man he had talked to looked after him with a sneer.

"Can take care of yourself, huh? Well, that wouldn't surprise me," he muttered. "But when the deck is stacked, my friend . . . " He lifted his shoulders. "Rogue wants you and a fella as won't be persuaded must be drove."

Striding down the street, he pushed open the door of one of the smaller saloons and entered. Three men sitting at a battered table with empty glasses before them, and a Mexican lolling behind the bar, comprised the company. The newcomer called for a drink and remarked aloud, with seeming irrelevance:

"Sure is a sorry sight."

One of the trio at the table, a craggy-faced fellow with greedy little eyes, looked up hopefully. "You said it, friend," he grunted. "But when gents is down to bedrock . . ."

The stranger laughed. "Oh, that's soon remedied," he said, and signed to the bartender.

While the glasses were being filled he studied the three men. He didn't know them, but he knew their kind. Hard cases, men who would slit a throat for a few dollars. Though they were drinking to him now, he knew they would rob him if they got the chance.

"You got me wrong," he explained. "What I was referring to was the sight of five hundred wheels getting ready to ride outa this town, to say nothin' of a fine black hoss with a white blaze, and a saddle the present owner shouldn't have much further use for."

Craggy Face looked up. "You tellin' us Sudden is around?" he asked.

"Just that," the other returned. "Saw him readin' the bill outside the Buckhorn; he was mighty interested too, and then he took off for Doan's livery stable. What do you guess?"

"If you're sure, why didn't you hold him up and—" Craggy Face began.

"Collect the dinero, huh?" the stranger finished. "Well, for one thing, he knows me, and there's another reason why I can't take any part in the affair."

He stressed the last six words and the listeners grinned understandingly: he was wanted himself, this hombre.

Craggy Face said, "Amounts to this; we take all the risk, and . . . "

"All the reward—I don't want none of it," he was told.

"I disremember if that notice said 'dead or alive.' "

"It did not, and I'm bettin' that Fourways fella ain't buyin' corpses."

Craggy Face emptied his glass and stood up, the other two following suit. Their informant added a word said, "I guess he'll take the western trail."

The hard cases nodded and went out. The stranger stayed for another drink and then did likewise, keeping well behind. After a while he saw the man he had betrayed jog-trotting along the street, heading—as he had guessed—for the western exit from town. Hardened as he was, he couldn't help admiring the young fellow's nerve.

His hat was slouched over his face; he appeared to be indifferent to his danger. But beneath the brim, his keen eyes scanned each passerby, alert for too much interest in himself. He did not expect an ambush, but the markings of the animal he rode were spelled out in the reward poster. So that he was not taken by surprise when three men, strolling aimlessly along the board sidewalk, abruptly swerved into the road in front of him. One of them yelled, "Put your hands up."

Jim did not hesitate, made no attempt to parley. Dropping the reins—already knotted for just such an emergency—over the saddle-horn, both hands came up holding guns. As they rose he fired both weapons, once, and his opponents on the right and left went down. Then, with a pressure of his knees, he jumped the horse at the man in the middle—Craggy Face. He cursed and tried to leap aside. He nearly succeeded, but the massive shoulder caught and drove him into the dust.

The whole affair had taken only a few seconds, but by that time the fugitive was two hundred yards away.

For some miles Jim rode hard, without looking back. The posse was less than half a mile behind and throwing all the lead they could. Jim felt the wind of a bullet on his cheek, others zipped through the brass beneath the flying feet of his horse. A cold fury flamed in him.

Dropping the reins, he pulled his rifle from the scabbard, twisted round in the saddle and flung four shots at the bunched-up posse. Two of the ponies went down, throwing their riders. A man reeled, clutched at the air, and pitched sideways to the ground. The posse pulled up. With a wave of defiance, Jim went over a ridge and down the other side.

He halted at last before a great chunk of rock, with a curious V-shaped crack dividing it as from a giant axe blow. The main trail—wagon-rutted—here turned sharply to the north, but westward there were hoofprints leading down into what appeared to be a welter of canyons.

"Split Rock," the Jim decided. "Well, old hoss, this is where we say goodbye to a law-abidin' life."

He sent his mount loping to the left, following the faint trail which plunged into the broken country. He came at length to the narrow mount of a gorge. Halfway up, on a ledge about thirty yards distant his eye caught a flash of steel.

"Stick 'em up, stranger; I got you covered," boomed a voice. A man with a leveled rifle rose into view.

Jim guessed this must be one of the outlaw sentinels. He had already decided on his own line of action, and though he halted, he did not obey the command to put up his hands. Instead he laughed satirically.

"I've had you fixed for the last two minutes. You oughta get that gun barrel dulled some—I saw it away back. Got any ideas?"

The other man knew he had been outplayed. On the strength of his leveled gun he had shown himself, but now he could see the drawn Colt nudging its owner's hip, and somehow, the rider of the black horse did not seem to be a person to take chances with. He decided to talk.

"What's your business here?"

"Any reason why I should tell you?"

"Only this," the man replied, tapping his rifle.

Jim laughed. "Hell, you'd miss and I wouldn't. Well, if it'll relieve your mind any, I'm lookin' for a fella called Rogue."

"I take it you're Sudden, then."

"You might be right at that. What about it?"

"I've had word to pass you along," the lookout admitted. "Go ahead. See you later—mebbe."

Half a mile farther on he rounded a bend and saw that the perpendicular sides of the gorge closed in; apparently there was no outlet. He had pulled up, and was studying the grey, weather-stained walls when a man stepped abruptly from behind a big boulder and directed him to the opening cleverly concealed by an outflung buttress of rock. Before him lay a beautiful little oval-shaped basin, the grass-covered floor of which sloped up on every side to an enclosing rampart of rock. In the center was a tiny circular lake. Cattle and horses were grazing near and on the far side of the valley were several log shacks.

He walked his horse to a shack some twenty yards away, in the doorway of which a man was standing watching the proceedings without apparent interest.

"Well, you got here—Sudden," he said.

The outlaw leader hesitated for a space, his hard grey

eyes studying the boy before him.

"I'm playin' straight with you, Sudden," he said, and the husky voice had a harsh note in it. "If you hadn't been in Fourways when Judson was killed they'd have picked on me, and I had Judson's money belt round my middle."

Jim sat up. "You did it?" he cried, jolted out of his impassivity.

"Yeah, but I didn't want to kill the fool," Rogue said. "I got the drop on him an' I'm steppin' in to take his gun when he jumps his hoss at me. I try to wing him but he's movin' you see, an' . . . " He shrugged his shoulders.

Jim was astonished that he should come face to face with the man who had committed the crime he was falsely accused of. "I was a plain fool to come into town but I figured him finished. I had to have the coin. Things have been quiet lately and the boys was gettin' restless."

"I saw them bills and knew they would close the towns to you," Rogue explained. "Reckoned you'd make for San Antonio and sent one of my men to watch for you.?"

"But it wasn't him sent me," Jim said, and told of the attempted arrest and chase.

If the outlaw smiled, it was behind his beard. He knew what had happened. His comment contained more than a touch of admiration: "Three fellas, with their guns out, and then you busted up the posse! You ain't losin' any time justifyin' your label, Sudden."

"My name's Jim—I'd rather you called me that."

"Mine's Roger, but everybody calls me Rogue and I dunno as I care. All the same, Jim goes with me. Now, you'd better stick around awhile, you're safe here. Now, there's another thing. Your face wouldn't look no worse without hair on it. Don't wanta part with that bronc, I suppose?"

Jim said no, not a chance." Rugue rummaged on a shelf and produced a bottle. "This dye'll wipe out them markings. I'll show you yore quarters."

He led the way to a little hut standing rather apart from the others. A man came out and grinned at Jim.

"This is Jim—he's aimin' to stay with us a piece," Rogue said. "You can put him wise and make him known to the boys."

The outlaw leader left them with a word that he would see them at supper.

"I'm Sandy," the man said.

two

Rogue was absent from the breakfast table on the following morning, but there was a new arrival in the person of the man Jim had seen in San Antonio. He grinned cheerfully at the cowboy and, when the meal was over, beckoned him outside.

"So you changed yore mind?" he said.

"You might call it that."

Well, you done right; San Antonio is shore a hot town. The sheriff ain't noways pleased. I'm tellin' you, better wipe that town off your list o' health resorts. Aimin' to throw in with Rogue?"

Jim did not reply at once. Despite the man's apparent friendliness, he did not like him. There was something mean about him.

"I ain't decided," he said, adding savagely. "What else is there for me to do?"

"Come ridin', that's what."

They went off laughing and the other man's eyes followed them sneeringly. "You got a lot to learn, the pair of you; a hell of a lot," he muttered.

They got their horses and separated, Sandy turning east to set free a man who was eagerly awaiting him, and Jim heading in the opposite direction.

The exit was easily found, a tunnel-like crack in the rim rock just wide enough to permit the passage of a mounted man. There was little light, for the cliff overhead appeared to be unbroken and the far end of the opening was masked by a mass of dense scrub. The few tracks showed that this means of entering or leaving the valley was seldom used.

Sandy had already told him that the nearest settlement on this side of the valley was some thirty miles distant, and that the only habitation of importance was the S-E ranch.

"Got a big range, has Sam Eden," the Sandy had said. "They say he owns a lot of the land too. Our village belongs to him but up to now he ain't served no writ of ejectment."

It was a wild bit of country into which Jim emerged. Every now and then, a fierce-eyed steer would break from a thicket, glare at the rider, and crash back into the brush. Some of these bore the S-E brand but more were unmarked.

"Sandy was right," Jim reflected. "Either Eden's outfit is damn careless or he ain't had a proper roundup in years. He can't holler if someone takes care of them mavericks."

As he was riding the rim of a shallow ravine, he heard a startled cry, followed by the beat of galloping hooves. It was a woman's voice and he judged it came from just ahead.

Along the bottom of the ravine, and only a few hundred yards away, a girl was desperately spurring her pony. A short distance behind, two mounted Indians were racing to overtake her. Jim pulled up, swung his horse round, headed it for the inclined wall of the fully, and leaned back in the saddle. The long leaping stride of the black soon began to overhaul the poorer animals in front, but Jim saw he had no time to waste, already the foremost Indian had grabbed the bridle of the girl's pony, and was endeavoring to drag her from the saddle.

She was resisting, striking at the savage with the butt of her quirt. Instantly the redskin whirled, dropped his lance, his right flashing to the quiver behind his shoulder, and Jim felt a searing pain at the side of his neck. The Indian notched a second, but Jim's revolver roared and the redskin pitched to the ground. His companion, seeing what had happened, abandoned the girl, flogged his pony savagely up the steep bank of the ravine—which it climbed like a cat—and, with a whoop of defiance, vanished over the edge. The cowboy followed, but by the time he reached the top the fugitive was half a mile distance on an open plain. When Jim returned the girl rode to meet him, a grateful smile on her firm lips.

"Thank you," she said, holding out a slim, gauntleted hand. Then, as her frank brown eyes studied this stranger she saw blood on the collar of his shirt.

"You're hurt," she cried.

"Not bad," he said. "Might as well make sure."

He rode back down the ravine, swayed easily over in his saddle to pick up the arrow which had grazed him, and examined it closely. Then he returned to scrutinize the contents of the dead Indian's quiver. He was grinning when he joined her again.

"Which I'm plumb lucky—that hombre grabbed a hunting shaft in his hurry," he told her.

Seeing that she didn't understand, he explained that the Indian had both hunting and war arrows with him, and that the flint heads of the latter were dipped in rattlesnake venom, making the least wound dangerous or even fatal. The girl shivered.

"We'll wash and tie up that scratch," she said, and though he protested, had her way.

"I'm Carol Eden," she told him. "The S-E ranch house in only about eight miles from here and my father will want to thank you."

"Why, there ain't no need—" he began, but she cut the protest short.

"He will think there is, and I agree with him. Besides, there may be other Indians about."

This was an unanswerable argument and again Sudden

had to give in; he was beginning to realize that here was a young woman who usually got what she wanted.

"You shouldn't be ridin' alone so far from home," Jim said.

"I know it. Dad warned me, but I thought the Indians were quiet now. I've been away East, at college, for some time."

"Injuns don't get quiet till they're like—him." Jim man said grimly, with a backward jerk of his thumb. "Dunno as you can blame 'em much—they've had a pretty raw deal. I'd oughta got that other; I've a hunch I'll be seein' him again."

"I hope I don't," the girl said.

To take her away from the subject he mentioned that he too had recently come back from the East. She looked at him with a new interest.

She went on to speak of herself. He learned that she was not really an Eden, the rancher having adopted her some years earlier, when the death of her father—his old friend—left her unprotected.

"He's been very, very good to me," she finished, softly.

But Jim was not as talkative. He told her his name and that was all. When she ventured a half-question, she received—as she had feared—only a half-answer.

"I'm just takin' a look at the country." he said.

"I'm glad you chose this bit of it today," Carol smiled. "We're near the ranch now. I must get ready for a tongue-lashing from Dad."

"He needn't to know," Jim pointed out. "You're safe now; I can fade—"

"No, I'll take my medicine," she told him. "You don't like your company?"

The cowboy's eyes crinkled at the corners. "I could bear to be with you a whole lot, ma'am," he said.

On the broad, covered porch, which extended along the

front of the S-E ranch house two men were sitting. The elder, short, big-shouldered, dressed in range rig, was Sam Eden, onwer of the ranch. The other man was of a different type. Baudry was by profession a gambler, though he was now sitting in a bigger game. His expresionless gaze studied the man before him.

"So you are going to take the chance, Sam?" he said.

"Sure I am—nothin' else for it," the rancher replied. "You see, Jethro, I want things clear for Carol—case anythin' happens to me, *sabe*?"

"You don't think I'd press her, do you?" Baudry asked.

"No, but yo're mortal too, an' gamblin' ain't the safest callin'," Eden replied bluntly.

"I can take care of myself," Baudry said with a thin smile. "Still, there's a chance. Setting that aside, you know I'm willing to wait?"

"Shore you've been mighty good lettin' me have the coin, Jethro," the rancher said warmly. "But think of it, man; a hundred thousand acres that, in a few years' time, may be worth as many dollars as I've paid cents for 'em. Wouldn't you wanta feel it really belonged to you?"

Actually the gambler was feeling just that, but his bland features expressed nothing of the greed which possessed him.

"Natural enough, but these big drives are risky they tell me," he rejoined. "You may lose your herd."

"I'm losin' 'em anyway," the cattleman said bitterly, and reading the question in the other's eyes, "Yeah, rustlers, of course. It's an easy play; the beasts are scattered in the brush and a lot must be unbranded; our roundups ain't been too thorough the last year or so—I couldn't afford a large outfit—and what was the use when all you could get for a steer was a few dollars for the hide and tallower? And for that you gotta drive 'em to a coast town, which cut the profit to near nothin' at all.

"You see, Jethro, durin' the war, the ranches were

neglected, the cattle ran wild, and the natural increase was amazin'. When the fightin' finished, every Texas cattleman found himself with more cows than he could count, and no market. Now, they tell me, it's different; the East needs beef; the gov'ment wants it to feed the Injuns on the reservations—when they can git the war-whoops to stay on 'em; the northern ranchers have discovered that the buffalo grass on their big plains will fatten cows and they're lookin' for stock. There's a shippin' point at Abilene, Kansas, and beasts worth little more'n nothin' here will fetch as much as fifteen dollars or more apiece."

"Certainly sounds good," the younger man said. "If you can make it."

"I gotta make it, or bust," Eden said grimly. "Anyways, you're sittin' pretty, Jethro; if I win through, you get your money; if I don't the ranch is yours; you needn't worry."

"I don't intend to," Baudry assured him, and again a fleeting smile swept over his pale face. Then he asked casually: "Any news of that son of yours?"

The rancher's brows met in a heavy frown. "I have no son," he said harshly. "When he went from here he stepped out of my life; I'll be glad if you'll remember that, Jethro." And, after a pause, "No, I ain't heard nothin'."

The other made no comment, but in his eyes there was a gleam of satisfaction.

"When do you expect to start north?"

"Soon as we can gather and road brand a sizable herd. Hello, who's that with Carol?"

The girl and her companion, having left their mounts at the corral, had suddenly appeared round the end of the ranch house. Baudry rose and bowed to the girl, who didn't seem too glad to see him.

"Dad, this is Mister Green, and I've brought him, much against his wish because I knew you would want to thank him."

In a few words she told the story of her adventure.

Sam Eden's hand went out. "Young fella," he said. "If there's anythin' I've got and you want, name it.

Jim gripped the proffered hand. "I happen to be handy."

Eden looked at the cowboy quizzically. "You don't happen to belong to that Rogue gang, do you? They got a hide-out round here somewhere."

Sudden shook his head. "I'm from south; havin' a look at the country."

The explanation satisfied the cattleman; he knew that the ranger rider was a restless animal, liable to fork his horse and set out, at short notice or none at all, in search of new country.

At the meal to which they sat down later, Eden asked Jim if he had any experience of trail-driving.

"Only short distances," Jim told him. "Never been north, but I hear it ain't no picnic."

The rancher nodded grimly. "Others have done it, and I'm goin' to," he said. "Like to come along? I can do with a couple more men." He saw the hesitation, and added, "Think it over—we won't be ready yet awhile."

Jim promised he would do so, and asked the probable size of the herd.

"I'm hopin' for three thousand head," Eden said. "Take some handlin' but I got a good outfit. The pay is thirty a month and every man gets a share when we sell the cattle.

Jim nodded. He liked the rancher. He didn't like Baudry. He didn't like the way he looked at the girl.

"Miss Carol, of course, will remain here," the gambler said.

"Miss Carol, of course, will—not," the girl said.

Her father looked at her in astonishment. "Don't talk foolish girl," he said. "There's no place for a lone woman on a trail drive."

Carol's reply appeared to be irrelevant. "Aren't you

taking Peg-leg?"

"Shore I am, we'd do fine without a cook, wouldn't we?"

"Then you'll have to take his wife—Judy won't let him go without her—so I won't be a 'lone woman,' you see." The rancher's face was clouding up but she did not wait for the storm to burst. "Can't I ride, rope and drive cattle as well as the boys?" she asked, and when he nodded a grudging assent, she added, "Well, then, you get a top hand for nothing, and you grumble. But of course, you were only teasing, you meant I should go all the time. I must tell Judy."

"I can handle the savagest steer or woolliest cowboy that ever forked a pony, but when it comes to what some funny fella called the 'weaker sex,' I'm beat," he confessed. "That bit of impudence does what she likes with me."

Jim left soon after the meal, returning the way he had come. The body of the dead Indian had vanished; his companion must have returned. The circumstance was to bear significance later, but now he gave it no thought. His brain was busy with the offer he had just received. It seemed to present a means of getting out of the mire into which chance had so unceremoniously thrown him, and moreover, the very enterprise itself appealed to his adventurous nature. The task of trailing three thousand wild cattle through eight or nine hundred miles of fierce, untamed country seemed worthy of a man. But he would not decide yet—he was a deliberate person. And because of that, he would not mention his afternoon's experience—even to Sandy.

"I'm bettin' he's straight," he told himself. "But our friendship is some recent."

When he reached the valley he found the men loafing outside the large cabin, smoking and yarning. Having disposed of his horse, he joined them. Rogue had apparently not yet returned. They watched him curiously as he seated himself on a bench next to Sandy, who was looking uneasy.

"Supper's through," that young man remarked, and then, in a whisper, "Suthin's up, dunno what, but watch out."

He had already sensed the air of expectancy with which his arrival had been greeted, and guessed that some attempt to "try him out" might be made. These men, desperadoes all, were not the sort to accept tamely a man on his reputation. He grinned.

Navajo and Ropey, standing six or seven yards away, were engaged in an argument, their voices rising. Sudden noticed that the other men were watching them. Presently Ropey, who was rolling a cigarette, snapped out an oath, and cried:

"Texas? I can tell you what I think of it right now. When a Texan dies, an' goes to hell—as they all do—he sure figures he's in heaven."

He had turned as he spoke and his narrowed eyes were glaring at the visitor. It was a direct challange, as all knew, and the chatter ceased. Jim, lounging on the bench, took no notice, and Ropey, with a grin of contempt, struck a match. Before he could apply it to the cigarette between his lips a gun flamed from the lounger's hip and the light was extinguished.

"What the hell?" the man gasped.

But Ropey had nothing to say; the fragment of wood remaining in his fingers appeared to hypnotize him. Jim said, "Any fella is free to damn Texas," he said, "but if he looks at me while he's doin' it, I take it as personal."

Ropey made a desperate attempt to save face. "I was only jokin'."

"Same here," Jim told him, with a cold smile. "If I hadn't been, I could have put your light out pretty permanent."

Later in the little cabin they were to share, Jim and Sandy referred to the incident.

"My Gawd, I never seen anythin' like it," Sandy remarked. "I ain't a mite surprised they named you 'Sudden.' "

"My friends call me 'Jim.' "

"I reckon this crowd'll think twice before it ruffles yore feathers again. Ropey ain't so bad. Navajo put him up to it—he don't like you—much."

"I got the edge on him there—I don't like him at all."

"See many folks on your ride?" Sandy asked presently.

"Well, I wouldn't say the country was thickly populated," was the smiling reply. "What's doin' tomorrow?"

"Like I told you, brandin', damn it. They fetched in 'bout three score mavericks this afternoon an' we gotta put the 8-B iron on 'em."

"Who owns that brand?"

"Couldn't say. There ain't no 8-B ranch around here that I knows of, but Rogue gets four dollars a head for all he can turn over."

Jim was surprised; this was legitimate enterprise, for in those days of free range, unbranded cattle were the property of the finder unless the real owner could prove a claim.

The explanation was to come in the morning, when the valley presented a scene of animation. A few hundred yards from the pool, a fire had been lighted, and to this each steer had to be dragged or driven, thrown and tied, while the hot iron was applied. Sudden found that he had been assigned the ticklish job of hog-tieing the victims. He had tied the first brute before he noticed the branded letters, S-E.

"Hey, this critter's got a label already," he said to Ropey, who came up swinging a long iron with a curved, red-hot end.

That individual grinned maliciously. "Well, well, fancy

that," he said. "Say, Navajo, the boys brought in one of Sam Eden's cows yestiddy: what we goin' to do about it?"

The half-breed slouched over. "Suppose we oughta take her back an' apologize, but I guess we won't," he replied, and grabbing the iron he added a few deft touches to the old brand, joining the ends of the S and the horizontal strokes of the E. "There, she's an honest-to-goodness 8-B now an' as cows can't talk, nobody'll know any different." He gave Jim an ugly grin. "Mistakes will happen, and I wouldn't be suprised if there's a few more."

The arrival of another steer, hauled by the ropes of two perspiring, blasphemous riders, ended the incident. From then on, Jim was kept busy, and, as he now expected, four out of every five of the cows he handled bore the S-E brand. So it was plain rustling. Nevertheless, he did his work with a thoroughness which earned reluctant approval even from Navajo.

"That *hombre* knows his job," he admitted to Ropey.

"Sure does," that worthy agreed. "Never seed anyone tie 'em so slick."

"Mebbe, but I don't like him," Navajo said.

"I'm plumb astonished," Ropey's said.

three

The outlaw leader returned that same evening, and from his cheerful mood, it was evident that his errand had been successful. After supper, he called Jim aside.

"Been helpin' the boys brand?" he asked casually.

"Been helpin' 'em blot brands," Jim corrected.

Rogue's brows ridged in a little frown. "You didn't think this was a religious community when you come here, did you?" he asked. "Shucks, what's a few cows anyway? I ain't keen on the rustlin' but it means somethin' to do and money for smokin'. I got a big thing on now, Jim, one that'll give you a chance of gettin' away for a time. Savvy?"

Jim nodded, and the other went on. "Here's the layout: Eden is takin' a hefty herd—three thousand head—north, and a fella I know is hopin' it won't get there." He smiled. "In fact, he's hopin' so hard that he's willin' to pay pretty handsomely if it don't, an' buy—at a fair price—all the S-E cows offered him."

"Failure to make the drive would bust Eden wide open, huh?"

"Yeah, it's his last hope, I reckon; he's been buyin' land and got in deep. But that don't concern me; a fella has to take care of hisself. Now, he'll want riders, and, I'm proposin' that you and Sandy get took on—can't use the other boys, their faces are known. You can see how it would help me to have a couple of men on the inside. We'll be on the heels of the herd and can keep in touch with you. Far as you're concerned, it gives you a trail outa present trouble and a tidy wad into the bargain. What do you say?"

"I'll drop in at the S-E in the mornin'," Jim told him. "Where do you aim to break the drive?"

"That'll depend on how things pan out, but not till they've got too far to come back and gather another herd," the outlaw said.

Jim found Sandy loading outside their shack. He told him about killing the Indian and rescuing the girl.

"Well, if you ain't the lucky one!" Sandy said. "Here's me been ridin' round for weeks and never had no chance to deliver a distressed damsel. Bet she's hatchet-faced, squint-eyed, and bellows like a sick cow.

"You musta seen the lady."

"I ain't—never knowed there was any female women in this neck of the woods. Who is she?"

"Sam Eden's daugher."

"She was stringin' you—he ain't got any."

"Adopted daugher, I oughta said—orphaned kid of an old friend," Jim explained, adding inconsequently, "Eden offered me a job."

"Goin' to take it?"

"We are," replied the other, and went on to tell of his talk with Rogue, and the part they were to play. Sandy listened carefully.

"Sounds good," he commented. "I'd sure like to be in on that drive, but Rogue's wrong in one thing—I ain't such a stranger around here." He thought awhile and then slapped his knee. "Got it!" he exclaimed. "Where's that stuff you used on your hoss?" he inquired.

"On the shelf inside," Sudden replied.

Sunrise found a grumbling cook giving them an early breakfast, but his curiosity regarding Sandy's black hair, eyebrows, and mustache remained unsatisfied.

"Ask Rogue about it," the boy told him with a grin, knowing perfectly well that he would do no such thing.

For the first few miles the pair rode in silence. It was Sandy who made the first remark:

"Odd I ain't heard of this gal at the S-E."

"She's recently arrived from the East—educated there, I gathered." Jim explained.

Sandy's next remark changed the subject. "I wouldn't be so terrible distressed if Rogue fell down on this drive-bustin'," he mused. "I don't owe him nothin' an' I sure would like to see them northern cowtowns."

Jim did not reply at once, he was wondering if the words had any hidden significance. His mind reverted to his own problem. What did he owe to Rogue? True, the outlaw had saved his life, but he had unwittingly done the same for him. And because of it, he was now a wanted man, afraid to show his face in any settlement. No, he decided, Rogue had not yet squared the account.

"I've a hankerin' thataway my own self," he confessed.

They reached the S-E ranch house to find it apparently deserted; the morning meal was over and the men had gone to their work. A hail brought Eden himself to the porch. At the sight of Sudden he called a hearty greeting.

"Hello, young fella, I'm main pleased to see you. Hope you aim to stay this time."

"Sure do, Mister Eden, if you'll have me," Jim replied. He pointed to his companion. "This is Dick Sands—he's huntin' a job too."

"Any friend of yours is welcome, Green, and I can certainly use another man," he said, but the warmth had gone out of his voice. "Well, boys, what's the word?" Eden asked.

"We'll go with you," Sandy blurted out eagerly.

"Good," the rancher replied. "Leave your war bags in the bunkhouse. There's plenty hosses in the corral—that mount of yores, Green, is too good for hazin' longhorns out of the brush." He pointed to a cloud of dust some miles away on the plain. "The herd is there."

He climbed briskly into his saddle and galloped away.

Sudden and Green chose horses and they soon reached the spot the rancher had indicated. Already about a thousand head had been assembled, and, kept bunched by a couple of riders, were grazing contentedly on the short grama grass which covered the plain. The herd was a mixed one; evidently everything in the shape of a cow was being rounded up, and the bellowing of the bulls mingled with the bleating of the calves as they staggered weakly after their mothers. At the moment Sudden and his partner approached, an addition of thirty animals arrived, convoyed by two riders who presented a striking contrast, one of them being tall and abnormally thin while the other was short and fat.

"Well, boys, you sure have been busy," Eden greeted them.

"Ain't all ours," the tall man explained. "Met Pebbles and the Infant, and took over their father."

"Here's a couple of fresh helpers, Jed. You better take Green, and Dumpy can put Sandy wise."

The four men rode away, and Jed said to Sudden, "We've pretty well cleaned up around here—have to go further afield."

Crashing into the underbrush further on, the riders unearthed a couple of steers and drove them into the open. Then, in turn, each guarded the "catch" while the other searched for additions. Both jobs demanded alertness and patience. The approach of evening found them with a collection of nearly two score.

"Pardner, we done noble," Jed said. "Reckon when we git 'em to the main herd we can call it a day."

"Suits me" Jim grinned. "I certainly hope you got a good cook; my belt's damn near slippin' off me."

In their search for cattle they had drifted some distance

from the plain and dark was creeping up by the time they reached the herd. The sight of a big fire and the nearby chuckwagon brought a doleful expression to Jed's face.

"Gotta sleep on our saddles tonight, seemingly," he said.

"You'll be some lucky if you sleep at all," a new voice put in. Another rider had caught them up—a wispy little man, nearing fifty, from whose brown face, wrinkled like a walnut, small blue eyes peered at the pair.

" 'Lo, Jeff," Jed greeted, and turning to his partner, added, "This is our foreman—a pretty ornery fella, as you can see, Green."

The little man chuckled and shoved out a paw. "Heard o' you from the Old Man," he said. "We can use you."

"And you'll find that's terribly true," Jed warned. "Say, Jeff, we got time to snatch a bite?"

Jeff waved toward the the brazing cattle. "The bunch is gettin' big and wants watchin', which is why we're campin' alongside. Also, Sam is in on the rampage; I reckon we gotta start *workin'* tomorrow."

"Sufferin' cats!" wailed the cowboy. "C'mon, Green, let's join the other loafers and load up before this slave driver makes it today."

Having unsaddled and turned their mounts loose—the beasts were too tired to stray far—they joined the group squatting round the fire.

"The holiday's over, boys," Jed announced. "Jeff was tellin' me we gotta start *work* tomorrow."

"Jee-ru-sa-lem!" someone said fervently. "That'll be a change, won't it?"

The foreman came up in time to hear the remark, and grinned as he delivered another blow:

"We begin road-brandin' in the mornin', boys."

Sudden had a word with Sandy. "We joined this outfit too soon," he said whimsically. "We'd oughta waited till they was ready to drive."

"I wish we hand't joined at all," his friend replied. "No, that ain't so neither, but—hell, what's the use?"

Soon after dawn the men were astir and crowding round the fire, for the early air was keen. Breakfast over, Jeff divided his forces; half were to begin the branding, while the other continued to build up the herd. Sudden and Sandy, as not knowing the range, were allotted to the first task, a decision which—to the former's surprise, met with his friend's satisfaction.

"We're shorely outa luck," he remarked tentatively.

"Suits me," Sandy replied gaily. "We'll show these *hombres* how to label longhorns."

The branding promised to be a big job. Chutes were unknown in the southwest of that day, and each animal had to be dealt with separately. Sandy found he was to work with his friend. Jim was waiting for him, a bundle of short tie-ropes in his hand.

"Hey," he called, "Yank some o' them bawlin' brutes over here and don't keep me waitin'."

"They'll come so quickly you'll get dizzy," Sandy promised. "I'll make you think it's rainin' cows."Jim smiled at the boast. While his was the more dangerous and tricky task, he fancied he could keep ahead of Sandy. But that optimist had helpers and soon the tie-man had his hands full. Cows bellowed and frightened calves blatted as they were hauled willy-nilly to the fire. The shouts and rough banter of the riders merged with the rattle of horn in the milling herd. Jim, looking up in a moment of respite, found Eden watching him.

"Good work, Green," he said, and as Sandy with a whoop rushed up another unwilling victim, roped and threw it, he added: Your friend seems to know his job, too."

He rode off without waiting for a reply, and Jim was glad; the praise worried him. He stole a glance at

Sandy—who was freeing his rope from the helpless steer—and was surprised to see that the boy's face was redder than even the fierce sun and his exertions warranted. He too, had heard what the cattleman had said.

"Damnation!" he growled, wheeled his horse, and vanished in a flurry of dust.

"You boys have certainly made a hit with Sam," the foreman commented as he pressed the hot iron home. "He ain't too fond of givin the glad word, neither, but he's a good boss."

Jim grunted an agreement. He liked the outfit, and its owner, and he was there to help ruin him. He tried to tell himself that the world, having made him an outlaw, was to blame for any consequences, but he could not make the argument convincing.

"Told you I'd make you hustle, didn't I?" Sandy said, a little later.

"Appears to me some other fella fetches along a steer now and then," Sudden replied, as he mopped his dirt-streaked face. "Say, I got an idea. You swap jobs with me tomorrow and you won't have to worry about shavin'."

"Nothin' doin'. Wouldn't change places with you for a blue stack."

Sandy shot off toward the herd and had almost reached it when he saw something which made him swerve suddenly; a nearly branded steer, mad with rage and pain, was rushing full at Carol Eden, who, intent on her chores, did not see it. With a yell of warning, Sandy raced and swung his rope. The loop dropped over the brute's horns and with a flip, he sent the slack over the rump and spurred his mount to the left, jerking the hind legs from under the steer. As it crashed down, the girl became aware of her danger and jumped her pony away. The fall had taken the fight out of the steer; as soon as the rope was removed it scrambled to its feet and lumbered off. Carol's face was pale.

"Thank you," she smiled. "I'm afraid you'll think I'm a tenderfoot to be caught like that."

Sandy's customary assurance had deserted him; he was the picture of confusion. Also, he was finding breathing difficult, for it had indeed been a near thing; had he missed his throw . . . He shuddered at what might have been.

"You are Mister Green's friend, aren't you?" she asked. He came to my assistance, too, so I'm now obliged to both of you. I ought to be glad you joined the outfit."

"I'm hopin' you will be," Sandy managed to say, and, as he saw his employer approaching, "Gosh, I'm forgettin' I got a job."

And he dragged a complaining calf on the end of his rope to the branding fire.

Days passed. The weather remained fine, feed was plentiful on the plain, and the branded cattle gave no trouble.

"For which, thank the Lord," Jeff said fervently. "If them critters took it into their fool heads to stampede, it'd be just merry hell."

Even when the herd was complete, much remained to be done. The big covered wagon, with its team of six mules, had to be overhauled and loaded with provisions. The remuda had to be selected—five horses for each man—weapons and ammunition prepared. Twelve men, including the rancher and the cook, were to accompany the herd, two older members of the outfit remaining behind to "hold down the ranch." These preparations entailed constant effort, for Eden was eager to start. So little did he spare his men that, but for the fact that he worked as hard as any of them, there might have been discontent.

Jim had little chance to converse with his friend during these days of stress, for the brief hours of rest were too precious to be wasted, but he got more or less acquainted with the other members of the outfit and decided that Sam Eden was a good judge of men. Rough, reckless, and shabby-looking in their coarse trousers, blue shirts and leather "leggin's"—they did not call them "chaps"—they were nevertheless capable. One only he did not approve of—a newcomer like himself—a big, dark, bewhiskered fellow named Lasker, who was in charge of a cow camp. He knew nothing against the man but instinctively distrusted him.

"He's got mean eyes," he explained to Sandy.

"Well, I dessay the horses won't mind," was the reply.

Jim looked at him thoughtfully. Sandy had changed since they had joined the S-E; his gay impudence had gone, to be replaced by a moody irritability. "He's pretty near played out, like the rest of us," was his unspoken reflection, but he knew it was not a satisfactory solution, for bone weary as all the men were, enthusiasm prevailed, whereas Sandy appeared disgruntled, sick of the whole business.

"Jeff tells me we're all set for an early start tomorrow," Jim said.

"It'll be a relief to get away from this blasted plain," was all Sandy had to say.

When the rancher and his daughter made their appearance in the morning they were accompanied by Baudry. Together they inspected the herd.

"They look good to me, but surely you have some oldish stuff amongst them," the gambler commented.

"Oh, I reckon they'll pass with the rest," Eden said. "You remember what the foreman of one of the early drives told the buyer who made the same complaint? 'Stranger,' he says, 'if you'd been through half what them critters has, you'd look twice your age.' "

Baudry laughed. "Well, you know your business, Sam, and I wish you all the luck there is," he rejoined. "I'll be coming north myself and shall expect to see you. Hear of the killing at Littleton?"

This was a settlement some thirty miles distant, and the

ranch having had no visitors was without news. Eden said as much.

"Coolest thing ever," Baudry went on. "A stranger steps into Greeg's saloon just after dusk, shoots the dealer at the monte table, collects all the cash in sight and backs out. When the company comes to life again, he's clean away."

"Another of Rogue's capers, I suppose?" the rancher said.

"They say not, unless he's got a new hand," Baudry replied. "From his looks, and a remark he made, he was Sudden, the Fourways and San Antonio killer." A rider on a big black horse, waiting to assist in starting the herd, caught his eye. "Why, that might be the fellow, by the description," he finished.

"What, Green?" the cattleman grinned. "He's been tied to the camp pretty tight the last two weeks. No, Jethro, there ain't no murderers in this outfit; Jim's all right."

"Jim heard the words but they brought him no satisfaction; the gambler's harsh voice had also carried to where he sat and the bitterness he had been trying to blot out of his life had overwhelmed him again. Another crime had been unjustly placed to his discredit. The world was determined that he should be an outlaw. Very well, since there was no other way . . .

He came out of his dark musing to find that the word had been given and the herd was already on the move, the point riders leading the way, the swing and flank men stringing the cattle out into a long line. Two men looked after the "drag," and behind came the remuda, in charge of the horse wrangler, and the wagon.

For the first week or so their trail would pass, for the most part, over the open plain, and Eden gave orders to push the herd hard so that it would arrive at the bedding-ground too tired to have any thought of breaking back to the thorny thickets from which it had been driven. In these early stages of the drive, twenty to twenty-five miles per day would be covered, to drop to half the distance later on.

Under the blazing sun the herd tramped steadily on. No great difficulty was anticipated until they crossed the Colorado River, the country south of that being familiar to most of the men. Nightfall found them camped near a little creek. For Jim riding moodily round the herd, watching first one and then another, sink down to sleep, the night brought only the opportunity to brood over his own troubles. Little more than half a mile away he could see the gleam of the campfire; if the men sitting round it knew who he was, they would hang him before dawn. And for this he had to thank Rogue, whom he was there to serve. Idly he wondered what the outlaw was doing, or about to do, and then swore savagely that he did not care. Which was not the truth.

Having watched the herd depart and waved an ironical farewell, Baudry turned his horse's head toward San Antonio. Five miles along the trail, squatting with his back against a spreading cedar, a man was waiting. Baudry got down, glad to avail himself of the shade.

"Well, Navajo, the S-E drive has started," he said. "What are Rogue's plans?"

The half-breed grinned unpleasantly. "You better ask him," he retorted. "His word was that he'd do the job—his own way."

The gambler's face reddened but he summoned a smile. "Suits me, so long as it's done," he replied. "Sam seems pretty confident.

"He ain't got a chance," the half-breed said.

"I think he has," Baudry said coolly. "In fact, I have so strong a belief in my friend Eden's courage and determination that I'd be willing to wager that he'll take his cattle through and return safely to his ranch."

Navajo laughed. "Sure you would," he sneered. "How much?"

"One thousand dollars."

"I'm takin' your bet. Give it to me in writin'—I got a shockin' memory." The jeer in the man's voice was insultint, but Baudry chose to ignore it.

"You needn't worry, I always pay my debts," he said.

Nevertheless, he wrote a few words in a notebook, tore out the page and passed it to the other. Navajo grinned as he tucked it away in a pocket.

"Money from home," he chuckled. "This ain't nothin' to do with Rogue, you savvy? So long."

The gambler stood watching his receding form, a heavy sneer on his thick lips.

"There's more than one way of paying a debt, you scum," he snarled. "When you've served your purpose . . ."

four

The Colorado River had been reached without incident, and the S-E drive was camped on the south bank waiting for daylight to make the crossiing. Supper was over, and the foreman, Jim, and several others were smiling beside the fire. There was a thicket to the right of the camp—the first timber they had seen for days—and the cook was busy chopping wood and loading it into the rawhide slung beneath the wagon.

"Well, trail-drivin' suits me. Why, it won't be no trick atall to push the bunch into Kansas." This from the gangling youth known as "Infant." The foreman surveyed him sardonically.

"Bein' a kid I suppose you gotta talk like one," he said. "If you think it's all to be like this you got another guess comin'. And that kind of yap is shore unlucky. Old Man Trouble always camps on the tail of a trail herd, and we'll hear from him soon enough without askin' for it."

"That's so," agreed another, who, being reputed to be the biggest liar in Texas, was called "Truthful." "I remember once . . . "

"Forget it twice," Jeff snapped. "What's come of Sandy?" He ain't with the herd!"

No one seemed to know. He had eaten with the rest of them and then slipped away. Jim had seen him go and smothered an impulse to follow because he had a feeling that Sandy had avoided him of late. He glanced round the camp, but there was no sign of the missing man. Against the dark background of the trees the little tent used by the women gleamed whitely. A few yeard away from it, San Eden leaned on the wagon tongue and chatted with the cook. Then, out of a thick tangle of bushes some forty paces from the wagon came a spurt of flame, followed by the vicious crack of a gun, and the sturdy figure of the rancher staggered and fell.

"Hell's bells!" Jeff cried, and ran to the stricken man.

The others followed, all save Sudden, who raced for the spot whence the shot had come. Noiselessly he searched, peering into the gloomy depths of the brush, listening for the snap of a breaking twig which would tell of a stealthy retreat, but he saw and heard nothing. Then came a careless foot step, a slouching figure swung into view and halted at Jim's curt command.

"Hello, Jim. What's the bright idea, stickin' up your friends?" asked a familiar voice.

It was Sandy, and despite himself, a note of suspicion crept into Sudden's question. "What are you doin' here?"

"Goin 'back to camp; what you reckon?"

"Where you been?"

"Pickin' flowers."

"Quit foolin', " Jim said sternly. "Sam Eden was shot from 'bout here less'n a quarter of an hour back."

"Sam—Eden—shot?" Sandy repeated. "God! And you're guessin' I did it?"

"I ain't doin' any guessin'," Jim told him. "I came to catch the skunk an' bump into you. Come clean."

"Is he hurt bad?"

"I didn't wait to see; Jeff an' some o' the boys is there. You ain't answered my question."

"I had nothin' to do with it, Jim," Sandy said hoarsely, "but it's likely I saw the fella. Mebbe ten minutes or so ago, a mere shadow slippin' through the bush. I didn't give it much attention—reckoned it was Lasker, goin' after his hosses—but it may not have been him at all. Hell! it'll break his gal's heart." Sudden's silence told him there was more to say. "You hear an owl hootin' while we fed?" he asked.

"Yeah, an' judged he was a pretty early bird," Sudden said.

The other nodded. "Overlookin' details like that'll land Rogue's neck in a noose some day," he remarked. "Yeah, I saw him."

Jim's eyes narrowed. "When did he leave you?"

"Mighty near half an hour back—I didn't hurry."

"Then he mighta done the shootin'?"

"Could have—he had time, but it don't fit with his plans."

"We better get back—it won't look too good for us to be absent and together," Jim suggested. "We'll have a pow wow later."

They had almost reached the camp when Lasker pounded up with a string of night horses. He stopped on seeing them.

"Heard about the Old Man being bushwacked, Lasker?" Jim asked.

The man's surprise seemed genuine. "Hell, no; who done it?"

"Your guess is as good as mine."

"With him cashed and the drive ends, I guess," the wrangler said.

"Who told you he's dead?" Jim asked quietly, and then, "Well, mebbe he is; we'll soon know."

The camp was very still. The other men had sought their blankets but the foreman sat near the fire, rifle beside him, his face a mask of worry. He looked up as the two friends approached; the horse wrangler was seeing to his charges.

"This is a terrible business, Jim," he said, and sensing the question uppermost in their minds, "No, Eden ain't cashed—yet. We got him bedded down in the wagon, an'

I've tended the wound—it ain't the first time I've played doctor. The slug went clean through and seems to have missed the vital parts. Plenty desperate, but might be worse. He's got a fightin' chance."

"Then he'll make it," Jim said confidently. "He's the fightin' sort."

"Beats me who the murderin' hound could be!" Jeff said.

"I went to see if I could catch him but didn't have no luck," Jim explained. "Sandy saw someone dodgin' through the brush and figured it was Lasker."

"Lasker, huh?" the foreman muttered. "Well, he's a new hand, but there ain't no reason. You boys better turn in—I'll be needin' you presently; gotta have four men watchin' the herd tonight."

It was two hours later when Jeff's low voice awakened them—in those dangerous days it was unwise to arouse a sleeper by touching him. They approached the slumbering herd slowly, exchanged a few words with the men they had come to relieve, and separated.

Jim was riding Thunder, for the night horse has to be the surest-footed, clearest-sighted, most intelligent of the cowboys' string of mounts. Knowing that the black would give instant warning of anything wrong, the rider allowed himself to think. The cold-blooded attempt to remove Eden had brought him definitely to the parting of the ways. He had little doubt that the outlaw chief had been concerned in it, and the thought of working with men capable of such a deed sickened him. The world had given him the name, but not the stomach of a desperado.

"With the boss in the discard, what's goin' to happen to the drive?" he asked himself.

Another point which worried him was the attitude of Sandy. "Eden's girl has him spellbound, and yet he's runnin' with Rogue," he mused. The two things did not seem to jibe and he resolved to clear the situation at the earliest opportunity. This came when, relieved in their turn, they were riding slowly back to camp.

"I'm puttin' a plain qucstion," Jim said. "Are you workin' for Rogue, or ain't you?"

"I'm givin' you a plain answer," Sandy replied. "To hell with Rogue, an' you can tell him I said so. You may be in his debt but I ain't. *Sabe*?"

Jim's laugh was bitter. "I'll tell you what I owe him," he said slowly.

Pacing side by side in the starlight, he could not see the listener's face but the muttered exclamations the story evoked showed his interest. When it was ended, Sandy drew a deep breath.

"My Gawd, you have surely had a tough break, Jim," he said, "I reckon all that's due Rogue from you is a slug of lead."

"It's past mendin'; even if I could prove I didn't kill Judson, the San Antonio affair an' this other, would hang me. Yo're ridin' with a shore-enough outlaw, Sandy."

"And damn glad to be," the boy said impulsively, thrusting out a hand. "I'm with you to the finish, Jim, whatever it may be."

Jim gripped the hand; it did him good to feel that he had a friend who, knowing all, trusted him.

"I'm obliged," he said simply. "When I joined the outfit my mind was all twisty-ways an' I didn't know what I was goin' to do. Now, I've got things straightened out; I'm on Sam Eden's payroll."

"That goes for me, too," Sandy rejoined. "We'll beat that gang of chaparral thieves yet."

Immediately after breakfast the foreman called a meeting of all the men in camp to discuss what should be done. Lasker was the first to speak:

"Nothin' for it but to turn back, far as I can see."

"Then your eyesight ain't what it oughta be," Jim put in. "I'm for goin' on; the Old Man'll want that, I'm bettin'."

Other opinions, for and against, were expressed, and in the middle of the argument a hail from the cook appraised Jeff that his employer wanted him. From his bed in the wagon the rancher glared at his foreman.

"What's all that chatter about?" he asked in a weak but angry voice. "Why ain't you startin' the herd?"

"We was sorta settlin' which way to go," the foreman excused.

"There's only one, you old fool—north," Eden snapped.

Jeff looked uneasy. "Well, you see, Sam, we figured you oughta have proper medical attention," he explained. explained.

Eden's pale face grew red with rage. "Medical attention, huh?" he sneered. "Do you reckon I've never been shot afore? Pretty fine outfit I got if you're goin' to turn tail an' run at the first bit o' trouble."

"That's not fair, Dad," Carol reproved. "They're thinking of you."

"You're right, honey," Eden said. "I didn't mean that, Jeff, but you can cut out the doctor talk—I don't need no help to die. And let me hear no more of goin' back; we'll take this herd through come hell or high water. Now, get them cows movin', or I'll be up an' see to it my ownself."

"And by Christmas, he'd have tried it," Jeff said when he reported the conversation to the others.

The only man who did not seem pleased was Lasker. "It's a fool play," he said sullenly. "He'll never make the trip—we'll have to plant him."

"All right, we won't ask you to dig the hole," Jeff retorted. "Take care of your hosses—we're surely goin' to need 'em."

Jim had a small investigation to make. In a patch of bare earth in the brush from whence the shot had come he found clear prints of a pair of moccasins, and scorched shriveled leaves showed where the weapon had been fired through the foliage. With a strip of rawhide he measured marks, making knots to indicate the width and length. His search for further footprints proved fruitless.

"Either made his getaway over grass or wanted them tracks to be seen," was his muttered conclusion.

Dismissing the matter for the moment he rode to the river, where preparations for crossing were in full swing. Conditions were favorable, shelving banks, and not much current. Already the cattle, grazed and watered, were being strung out and headed for the stream. Jeff, bawling orders right and left, was watching the operation.

"Shouldn't be difficult to get the cows and hosses over—the river's lower'n I ever see her," he remarked. "That damn wagon'll be the troublemaker; with Sam and the women aboard she'll be overweighted for floatin'."

"How about stringin' a stout log along each side?" Sudden suggested. "Oughta help keep her outa the water."

"That's an idea," the foreman admitted, and dispatched a couple of men to cut down trees.

"Don't rush 'em boys," the foreman instructed. "Haze 'em along gradual-like but keep 'em movin'. We want to be over before the sun gits too high, and these damn streams is liable to rise mighty sudden."

There was little trouble; the leading steers, when they felt the cold water sweeping beneath their bellies, tried to retreat, but the watchful riders, with quirts and the ends of their ropes kept them from turning and soon they took the plunge and swam steadily for the opposite bank.

The crossing took time but went without a hitch, and Jeff breathed a sigh of relief when the last steers climbed the far bank, shook themselves, and went to grazing peacefully. The remuda followed, and then the wagon came lumbering up, a sizable trimmed tree trunk lashed along each side. Drawn by its full team of six mules, it rocked and slithered down the slope to the stream. The leaders balked at the water but the biting lash of the long whip stung their flanks and threw them into the collars again. With a final lurch, the clumsy vehicle slid into deep water and, to the relief of all, floated. With a couple of riders on either side steadying it with their ropes, the wagon proceeded slowly across, to be greeted with a cheer when the dripping team hauled it safely up the bank.

"One less river, one less river to cross," chanted the Infant, as he detached his rope, turned his mount loose, and lay down to let the sun dry his pants.

The foreman, who had followed the vehicle over, poked his head through the flaps at the back. "How'd she go, Sam?" he asked anxiously.

"Fine—never jarred me none," the invalid lied stoutly. "Get agoin' soon as you like; it does me good to feel we're movin'."

The long line of men and beasts moved like a sluggish stream over the apparently unending area of brown, sun-dried earth, cracked and fissured by the fierce heat.

Uneventful days had slid by since they crossed the Colorado, and the outfit was making the most of an easy time. Even the foreman's lined, leathery countenance wore an unwonted smile as he rode to Jim's side and nodded at the surrounding scene.

"All like this and it'd be easy, but it ain't goin' to be," he remarked. "We got most of our trouble ahead of us."

Jim told of the moccasin mark and mentioned the Indian who had escaped when he rescued Carol. Jeff shook his head.

"Might be, of course, redskins is vindictive devils, but I don't think it and neither do you," he said shrewdly.

To this the other made no reply. He was studying the broad, trampled track they were following.

"You figure this John Chisholm's trail?" he asked.

"I'm hopin' so. Anyways, she's good goin' and pointin'

north, which is all we want," Jeff told him.

That evening, before supper, Jim drew Sandy apart.

"What did Rogue tell you of his plans?"

"Nothin' definite, but I gathered that he aimed to hold up the herd; get what coin he could outa Eden, bust up the drive later on, and collar the cows. It's a-plenty."

"Sure is," Jim said soberly, and then his eyes twinkled. "I'm takin' it you don't still propose to help him in them projects?"

"Your damn right," the boy returned hotly. "and the sooner he knows it the better."

"That's somethin' we'll let him find out," Sudden decided. "Our hand'll be hard enough to play without showin' it."

Cheerfulness was in evidence at supper that evening; the easy going and the improving health of the wounded man had put everyone in a good humor.

Early on the following morning the camp had visitors, six mounted men, well-armed, and range-riders by their rig. One, who appeared to be the leader, signed to the others to halt, and rode forward. Peg-leg was busy loading his vehicle for the day's march. Carol, who had just mounted her pony to join the herd, halted at a word from Sudden, the only other man in camp.

"Tell Jeff to fetch in some o' the boys," he told her. "I ain't likin' the look of these *hombres*."

The girl nodded and rode away. Sudden waited, his fingers concerned with a cigarette but his eyes taking in the newcomer.

"Mornin'," Jim said laconically.

The other man returned the greeting, adding brusquely, "Whose outfit is this?"

"You got any right to ask?" the S-E rider retorted.

The visitor shot a glance at his escort and smiled grimly. "I reckon," he replied. "A 'full-house' always beats a 'pair,' " with a significant look at the other's guns.

Jim smiled too. "We ain't come to the 'draw' yet," he said. "However, if it'll ease your mind any, this is the S-E from San Antonio way drivin' north, and I don't like talkin' to a fella on a hoss when I'm afoot."

"Fair enough," the stranger replied, and got down, keeping his horse between himself and the cowboy—in itself a hostile action. "I wanta see the boss."

"He's sick. I'm speakin' for him. You ain't told me who I'm talkin' to yet."

"Name's Dale, foreman o' the Double O; you're nearly across our range now."

Jim weighed the answer and found it wanting; they had seen no cattle bearing that brand. Out of the corner of his eye he saw an approaching dust cloud and knew that help was on the way.

"What's your trouble?" he asked.

"Ain't got none, but your herd musta picked up quite a few of our cows and we want 'em back. *Sabe*?"

The S-E man did. It would mean a couple of days' delay, to say nothing of the hard work involved. He wondered if this was one of Rogue's moves. He did not know who the man before him was, and the others were too far off and had their hat brims pulled down.

"We ain't seen any Double O cows," he said.

"The outfit ahead of you told us the same and we found near a hundred when we combed the herd," Dale countered.

In a flurry of flying sand, Jeff and four riders pulled their panting ponies to a stop. The foreman was on the point of riding forward when Sandy put in a word:

"Leave it to Green. I'm bettin' he can handle it—now."

The fact that the sides were no longer unequal brought a change in Jim's attitude, but he showed no hostility.

"We ain't got time to waste," he said. "Anyways, what you gotta grumble about? We're drivin' north, where cows—they tell me—is worth four or five times what you can sell 'em for here. You'll be paid what it fetches for every Double O steer we find, an' we won't charge you nothin' for handlin' 'em either."

"Mighty generous," Dale sneered. "Now I'll make you a better offer. Call it fifty of our beasts you got, which is lettin' you off easy. Well, pay me ten dollars a head for 'em now, an' when you sell you get a nice profit. How about it?"

Jim laughed at him. "Didn't I tell you we're from the South?" he asked. "Where'd we raise all that coin, do you reckon?"

"We'll 'cut' your herd, then," Dale said angrily. "It's that or fight." He glanced at Jeff and his companions. "I've got more men within call."

"You'll need 'em," Sudden told him. "But where's the sense in a ruckus which may cripple two outfits? Here's me, and there's you; why not state a case for Judge Colt and settle it between ourselves?"

Through his slitted eyelids the Double O foreman glared at the young fellow who had so coolly challenged him to single combat, and now stood, teetering on his heels, waiting for an answer. There was a sardonic, almost hopeful, gleam in the half-veiled grey-blue eyes; the butts of the two guns were shiny with use; the hand that lifted the cigarette to the firm lips was as steady as a rock. Dale had killed several times, was noted for his speed with a six-gun, and nothing would have given him greater pleasure than to shoot down this obstacle to his plans, but doubt assailed him, and he evaded the issue.

"You talk about sense," he sneered. "Why not show some and let us take our cows like them fellas in front of you?"

"How long was you cuttin' 'em out?" Sudden asked casually.

"Coupla days," was the answer.

"They were that much ahead of us, and we ain't been

delayed," the S-E man said musingly. "Funny we didn't catch 'em up, ain't it?"

Too late Dale saw the trap he had stumbled into. His face flushed as he said savagely:

"Meanin' I'm a liar?"

"Just that," Sudden told him, half-turning as though the interview was ended.

Passion swept the other man's caution to the winds, and he did not stop to think that he had been jockeyed into doing what his opponent had already proposed.

"Why, you damned young squirt," he rasped, and grabbed at his gun. He got it clear of the holster but before he could press the trigger there came a flash and a roar from Jim's side. Dale dropped his weapon and clutched a ripped forearm.

"You ain't hurt much and you got another gun. If you're wishful to try the left hand . . . "

The Double O man looked at him, stark hatred in every line of his face. He was nearly mad with pain and humiliation, and for an instant, it seemed he might take up this second challenge.

"I'm advisin' you not to," Jim said quietly. "Further south, they call me Sudden."

The fellow's eyes widened and something very like fear took the place of the ferocity in them. He picked up his pistol, and grabbing the horn of his saddle with his left hand, hauled himself up.

"We'll be meetin' again and mebbe I'll be lucky," he growled.

"You've been lucky this time," Jim replied. "Keep on thinkin' that. Now roll yore tail, and take that bunch of trail robbers with you."

Watching them ride away, he became aware of Jeff at his elbow asking what is was all about. The foreman's face when he heard the particulars was a picture of puzzlement.

"Mebbe we have got some of their cows," he suggested.

"Shucks, then we can turn over what they fetch," Sudden argued. "Any of you boys seen the Double O brand?"

Not one of them had. "Me neither, and I've been lookin' pretty constant for strays," Jim went on. "I'd risk a little that there ain't such an iron hereabouts—his horse wasn't wearin' it. No, sir, it was a plain holdup."

"If they'd combed the herd and hadn't found any . . ." the foreman speculated. "Why should they want to hang up our drive?"

"These holdup gents will be watchin' the used trail," the cowboy pointed out. "Suppose we were to bear away to the west for a spell and then strike north again, nosin' out a road for ourselves; wouldn't that razzle-dazzle 'em?"

"It'll mean a longer and harder drive, but that'll be better than losin' men scrappin', and it's possible Chisholm didn't pick the best path after all. Now, go and get them steers started."

Notwithstanding Jeff's approval, Jim did not feel too comfortable. The step he had suggested was dangerous and might well plunge the expedition into all kinds of difficulty. On the other hand, there was the chance that it would dislocate Rogue's designs on the drive, and this had been his main reason. That Dale was one of the outlaw's men he felt sure, and he was relieved by the thought that he had now declared himself.

The new plan was not to be put into operation immediately, and dusk found them camped again on the trail they had been following. They had another visitor that evening. The herd had been bedded down, four men left in charge, and the others were grouped around the fire awaiting Peg-leg's intimation that supper was ready, when a figure materialized out of the gloom and came toward then, right hand raised, palm foremost.

"Evenin', folks," greeted a high, reedy voice. "Saw

your fire an' it made me feel kind o' lonesome."

"Step right up, friend," the foreman called out.

The man came on, moving with the easy, tireless stride of redskin. His tattered doeskin garments, raccoon-skin cap, and moccasins proclaimed that he was a trapper.

"Sit an' eat," the foreman invited.

"Thankee," the stranger replied. "But I pay my footin'."

He lifted the long gun from shoulder and proffered the carcase of a small deer slung upon it. Jeff protested, but the visitor would not listen. When the food arrived he ate so wolfishly that even in a land of large appetites he knew it must be remarked.

"You gotta excuse me, friends," he said, "but you have one damn fine cook, an' I've been livin' on straight meat an' water for most a week; run right outa meal, salt and coffee."

"I guess we can fix you up," the foreman said. "Goin' far?"

"Makin' for the nearest settlement to trade my pelts for supplies," the stranger explained. His name, he said, was Tyson, and his story a common enough one in those days. Just a tale of ravaged cabin, a murdered wife and children and another blood debt to the shrieking painted devils who had wrecked his life. He told it quite simply in his high-pitched voice, without passion, but in his eyes smoldered a hatred which only death would quench.

The foreman questioned him regarding the country for which they were heading, and the chances of getting the herd through.

"Middlin' slim," he said bluntly. "You'll have a man-size job to make it. Steers is bringin' real money at the railhead, and it's knowed that herds is comin' up from Texas. The Nations is lousy with bad men, hide hunters, rustlers, outlaws of every sort, an' they ain't likely to overlook a bet of that kind. Then there's the Kiowas an'

Commanches from the headwaters of the Red River; they're watchin' the trail mighty close."

"Suppose we turned west for a piece and then cut our own road north?" Sudden queried.

Tyson grinned. "She ain't a bad idea—might diddle 'em," he admitted. "But you gotta mind you don't hit the Staked Plain—no water and hot as Hell's gridiron—an' if your cows get tangled up with a herd of buffalo you can wish 'em goodbye. All the same, I'd say it's your best bet."

Soon after midnight, Jim—having done his turn of night-herding, returned to camp and sought his blankets. He had not fallen asleep when he heard the low, musical but melancholy hoot of a dwarf owl. Since there were not trees or bushes in the vicinity, the presence of the bird was sufficiently remarkable to call for investigation. Slipping from beneath his covering he crawled cautiously in the direction from which the sound had come. Again he heard it, and smiled; clever as the imitation was, he felt sure it was the product of a human throat. At the side of a small hummock he stood up, drew his gun, coughed slightly, and instantly moved.

"That you, Sandy?"

"No it's Green."

A shadow detached itself from the side of the hummock.

" 'Lo, Jim, I was wantin' a word with one o' you," Rogue said, and then, abruptly, "Why did you shoot up my man, Dale?"

"How in hell was I to know you owned the Double O brand?" Jim said.

"I don't," the outlaw chuckled, "but you mighta guessed how it was. Bad luck he had to bump into you."

"I'd say he was plumb fortunate," Jim retorted. "Next time he starts to pull a gun on me he won't get off with just a busted arm."

"It looks like you mean to doublecross me, Jim," Rogue

said harshly.

"Doublecross nothin'," was the reply. "I never joined you, and I don't owe you anythin' but a bad name and a prospect of swingin' for a crime you committed."

The savage intensity of his tone seemed to impress the other and when he spoke again the rasp had gone from his voice:

"That's so. I got you in bad, but I did what I could to get you clear. I liked you, Jim, an' when you were ready to join the S-E I reckoned it meant . . . "

"That I was ready to be what you had made me—an outlaw," Jim finished bitterly. "Well, it mighta been—I was undecided—but when it came to shootin' old men from cover . . . "

"I had nothin' to do with that, Jim."

"You were around when it happened."

"I'd gone. I knew afterwards, but it was no part of my plan."

"Then who did it?"

"I don't know who fired the shot, but Navajo fixed it. I had trouble with him over that—and other things. He's gettin' uppity."

The cowboy was silent, considering. Somehow he believed Rogue was telling him the truth. Outlaw he undoubtedly was, yet he possessed a streak of something—bravado, it might be—which made him scorn a lie as the resort of a coward. He had been frank over the killing of Judson, when he need not have been.

Rogue said, "Must be gettin' tired holdin' that gun, Jim; there ain't no manner of need."

Shame swept over Jim as he slipped the revolver back into its holster. "Sorry, Rogue," he said.

"Shucks," the outlaw said, and there was a weariness in his tone. "I don't blame you for playin' safe, boy. I'm taking' it I can't count on you and Sandy?"

"That's correct," Sudden told him. "We ain't neither of

us bitin' the hand that feeds us."

"Bite on this, boy; I've passed my word to bust Eden's drive and I'm goin' to do it."

"And I'll fight you till hell freezes." Jim smiled, and shoved out his hand. "No hard feelin's, Rogue, but that don't go for your followin'. *Sabe*?"

The bandit gripped the hand heartily. So this strange compact between men who were to war, one against the other, was sealed. The intruder melted into the shadowed plain and Jim crept back to the camp, his mind full of the man he had just left. For the interview had surprised him. He had gone to it expecting reproaches, threats, even attempted violence, and found none of them. That the outlaw was of a superior type he now recognized and wondered what trick of Fate had set his feet to tread the crooked path of crime. He had given his promise to his employer and would do his best to fulfill it. As to who this might be, Sudden could make no guess; Sam Eden's outspoken nature and quick temper would earn him enemies enough.

His thoughts veered to the dark, sinister face of Navajo, the man who—according to Rogue—had "fixed" the attempted murder of the cattleman. Was it a misguided effort to help his leader, or was the fellow playing a hand for himself?

five

The days oozed by, days of long, lazy hours in the saddle under a scorching sun. Jeff was too good a cowman to hurry the herd but he took care that the animals were healthily tired and ready for sleep when they reached the camping place: from twelve to fourteen miles a day was a good average.

"Everythin' is goin' too slick—it ain't natural," Jeff grumbled, pacing behind the wagon. "Just when yo're feelin' careless an' contented is the time Lady Luck chooses to give you a kick in the pants."

The cattleman pulled a wry face. "If you was lyin' here you wouldn't think it was all so hunky, you ol' death's head," he replied. "How're the new men pannin' out?"

"Green an' Sands all right but I don't like Lasker," Jeff said bluntly. "Does his work but . . . " He did not finish. "Wish I knowed who put that pill in you, Sam."

"You ain't thinkin' it was one of the outfit, are you?"

"I'm in the dark," the foreman admitted. "Sandy or Lasker could have done it—they weren't in camp or with the cows."

"Forget it," Eden said irritably. "I'm here, ain't I? Why should any of the boys want to crab the drive? I figure it was a war-whoop, the one that got away from Green, likely; Injuns never let up when it's a case of evenin' a score."

Probably you're right, but I'm—wonderin'," Jeff insisted. Quickening his pace, he rode after the herd. As he passed the remuda, he spoke to Lasker:

"We must be near Injun country now. Best not let yore hosses stray far tonight. You can have help if you want it."

The wrangler nodded sullenly. "I can manage," he said.

"Been this way afore?" Jeff asked.

"Nope, it's new to me," the man replied. "What do you make of that sky?"

The foreman's gaze followed the pointing finger. On the northwest horizon great masses of cloud were piling up—thunderheads and moving rapidly toward them. The cattle ahead of them, bawling incessantly, appeared nervous and frightened. One glance was enough for Jeff.

"Hell's delight!" he spat out. "If she breaks we'll have one busy time. Keep them broncs together and close to the herd. Tell Peg-leg to watch out."

He spurred his horse along the line, yelling directions. The drag men were ordered to hurry up their charges, and then the foreman shot ahead to stay and turn the leaders.

"Get 'em bunched an' millin' before the storm starts," he said. "It's our only chance of stoppin' a stampede, and a slim one at that."

Carol cantered up. "What can I do, Jeff?"

"Race for the wagon and get inside," he said, and when she protested that she wanted to help, added, "You'd only be another worry, girl, and Sam'll want you with him."

She obeyed without another word, and Jeff went to assist the point riders, who, with shouts and quirts, were turning the head of the herd upon itself, driving the frightened beasts back to meet those still coming on. Fortunately the cows were now "trail-broke" and having nearly completed the day's journey, were too tired to be obstreperous.

The foreman's maneuvre proved succesful and by the time the storm actually reached them the cattle were massed, still moving, but slowly and in a circle. The sky was now black with great rolling waves of clouds, the sun had gone, and both men and beasts shivered in the breath of an icy wind which bit to the bone. Then came a flare of white flame which lit up the whole plain, a shattering peal of thunder, and a volley of frozen rain. Madly the riders circled the herd; if they could hold them under the first onslaught there was a chance. The clashing of horns, squeals of scared steers, shouts and oaths of dripping, darting horsemen were added to the pandemonium Nature had already provided.

Smarting from the sting of a myriad icy pellets, dazzled by the incessant flashes of lightning which played on their horns and backs like a phosphorescent flame, and crazed by the deafening explosions overhead, it was inevitable that the poor beasts should make some effort to escape. Jim saw the movement just in time and spurred the big black headlong in the path of the culprits. Half a dozen shots across their noses sent them wheeling again from the new danger, and with Sandy's help, they were soon back in the herd, to stand, heads down, tails to the tempest.

Soaked to the skin and chilled to the marrow, the riders watched their charge as a miser might his gold. Anxious eyes scanned the sky, and it was with relief they saw the storm was passing. The glare of the lightning and cannonade of the thunder were lessening, the hail had become a cold rain, and on the horizon behind the scurrying, inky clouds, was a gleam of reappearing brightness. The foreman wasted no time.

"Get 'em goin', boys," he ordered. "And push 'em along."

Two or three miles were covered and their eyes were gladdened by the sight of trees in the far distance. They knew the line of foliage indicated a river.

"Reckon that'll be the Red," Jim remarked to Sandy. "I'm wonderin' what that damn storm has done to her—it must have come from the headwaters."

"She'll be high," Sandy predicted. "We got off too light in that flurry—bound to be a hangover."

Their fears proved to be well-founded, for when, a little later, Sudden and the foreman—who had ridden ahead—halted on the bank of the river, they saw that the storm had indeed left what Sandy had termed a "hangover." Jeff's face fell as he surveyed the swift-moving, eddying torrent, murky with the red sediment which stained the timber and driftwood along the banks and gave the river its name. He shook his head.

"She's all of six hundred yards acrost and with the drift that means swimmin' near twice as far, and she's carryin' too much sand," he said. "We'll never make it as the cards lie."

"Better play it safe, oldtimer," Jim agreed. "These streams, I've heard, rise and fall in a day."

He was studying the ground; there were cattle tracks in plenty.

"Suppose them jaspers in front of us beat the floodwater, but I'm guessin' they didn't cross here," he remarked.

"They may still be on this side—further downstream," the foreman suggested. "The trail forked a few miles back. Well, we gotta wait, whether Sam likes it or not."

The bedding-down of the herd on a small plateau well away from the river gave no trouble, thanks to the spell of sunshine after the storm, for cattle will not lie on wet grass. The wagon was drawn up beneath some tall pines, and the cook was busy with his pots and pans when a horseman rode in from the gloom. Jim, watching the leaping flames of the big fire, stepped forward.

"This Sam Eden's outfit?" the new arrival queried, and then, peering from his saddle, "But of course, it must be, unless yo' riding for someone else. Isn't your name Green?"

Sudden did not reply. Directly the rider had come within the circle of firelight he had seen that it was Jethro Baudry, and for some reason he did not attempt to track down, the aversion he had experienced on first meeting the man returned.

"And where is Sam? Not working while his men warm their hands, I hope?" Baudry went on.

"You'll find Mister Eden in the wagon," the cowboy said stiffly, and walked away.

He rode over to the wagon, got down, and looked in. By the light of the hanging oil lamp he saw the invalid, pale and haggard, but obviously on the mend.

"Hello, Sam, what's the meaning of this?" he greeted.

The visitor listened in silence to the story and then gave his opinion:

"Looks like redskins, who else would want to lay you out?"

"You can search me. But how come you're here, Jethro?"

"Meeting a man at Doan's store—some way down the river. Got news of a herd arriving and suspicioned it might be the S-E. You're making good time, Sam."

"Barrin' this," Eden tapped his chest, "we've been lucky. Mebbe all our troubles is to come."

"Likely enough, and that's one reason I wanted to see you," Baudry said. "I've been told there's some pretty tough gangs haunting the trail, waiting for herds, and I thought I'd warn you to be on the lookout."

"Might good o' you, Jethro," the rancher said warmly. "I've had word already to the same effect,but—" his eyes twinkled"—"if they wait for the S-E they're liable to get tired of the job."

Baudry looked puzzled.

"We're aimin' to turn west and cut our own trail," Eden explained triumphantly.

"You're a sly old fox, Sam," the gambler said. "But isn't it risky? You may euchre the rustlers but you'll certainly run into the redskins."

"I figure them varmints will be watchin' the trail too," the cattleman argued. "As for bein' risky, the whole damn drive is that. Seen anythin' of another herd this way?"

"Yes, they crossed some miles lower down—just beat the flood. The river's dropping—you'll get over tomorrow, I'd say."

"Hope so. I fair hate hangin' about. Comin' with us, Jethro?"

The gambler shook his head, and rose. "Have to wait for my man," he said. "I'll be seeing you later. Good luck to you, Sam."

The river next morning showed an appreciable fall but there still was a vast volume of reddish, sand-laden water sweeping swiftly between the bluff banks, and to the group of men studying the swirling currents it was clear that the crossing would be a difficult and perilous undertaking.

"I guess we gotta take a chance, boys," the foreman decided. "Another storm an' we might be held up here for days. What's yore opinion, Jim?"

"She's a gamble, with the odds against us," was Jim's verdict. "But we've played in luck, so far."

The foreman had already made up his mind and presently the leaders of the herd appeared, trotting briskly, for in view of the crossing they had been kept thirsty. At the sight of the turgid flood, however, they balked and would have turned but for the riders on both flanks, who with shouts and epithets drove them into the water. There they stood, knee-deep, snorting and bawling with fright, the forces of the stream almost sweeping them from their feet. Beyond this they would not budge until Sudden splashed in, roped the foremost steer round the horns, and slipping the other end of his lariat across the broad breast of thunder, headed for the far bank.

Willy-nilly, the captive was dragged head-long into the flood and struck out lustily, seeing which—after a brief hesitation—those behind followed. In a few moments, a steady string of horned heads was moving across the river. Then came one of those causes of calamity the trail driver always had to expect. A fitful puff of wind whipped the surface of the stream into waves and flung them in the faces of the leading steers. Instantly they attempted to retreat but the quirts of the accompanying cowboys prevented this, and when the animals saw their leader majestically proceeding through the broken water, they too went on. Jim, having pulled his victim up the far shore, removed the loop, and grinned at the disgruntled-looking brute, which seemed disposed to go "on the prod."

The foreman met him, his face beaming. "Jim, that was a daddy of an idea," he said. "You sure know cows."

"Shucks," Sudden smiled. The critters is like humans—give 'em a lead and they'll go most anywheres."

"Say, Jim do you figure we've razzle-dazzled Rogue?" Sandy asked.

"Mebbe, but he's a foxy fella and now he knows we ain't workin' for him he's probably trackin' us," Jim replied. "But I expect we've put one over on other gents watchin' the trail."

They were riding some five hundred yards ahead of the herd, for being in Indian territory, scouts were deemed necessary, and, since they were no longer following a used trail, the easiest route had to be selected. More than a week had passed since they left Red River and during most of the time they had traveled westward before turning north again. Not one of the outfit had more than a vague notion of their location, for save to the Indians and a few trappers and buffalo hunters, this was unknown country.

"Plenty lonesome in these parts," Sandy remarked presently. "We ain't seen a soul since the Red."

"Suits me," Jim said. "Anybody we met would likely be hostile."

The foreman agreed to call it a day, camp was made near

a thicket of oak and mesquite, while the cattle were bunched on the flat top of a swell not far away. There was no water but the animals had had enough the night before, and the longhorn could travel forty-eight hours without drinking. Nevertheless, the lack of it made the herd restive and Jeff anxious.

"You look as happy as a wet hen," Sandy said to Jim. "What's bitin' you?"

"I dunno, Jim, and that's a fact, but I got a feelin' trouble is comin'."

"Trouble always is comin' and worryin' won't stop it. Get such fool notions outa the thing that holds your hat up, and keep a close eye on them durned cows; half of 'em ain't even dozin' yet."

"They're missin' the water," Sandy said. He glanced at the sky, in which only a few faint stars were showing. "She's a gaudy night for a stampede."

"Close your trap, you red-headed misery," Jim grinned.

Riding back to the camp he heard the mournful, weird howl of a coyote and a moment later came an answering cry. He pulled up in doubt; to his trained ear they did not sound just right. Smiling sardonically at the reflection that Sandy had made him nervy, he nevertheless circled to approach the rear of the timber behind the camp, whence the cries had seemed to come. This took some time, for the thicket was larger than he had thought and it was incumbent to move cautiously. Reaching the trees, he sat listening; the indistinct mutter of a voice came to him. Slipping from his saddle, he crept into the undergrowth. It was nervous work; once he put a hand on a clammy, writhing form and heard a sharp hiss as the repitle slithered away. Jim shivered.

"Fools for luck," he murmured. "If rattlers didn't have to coil afore they can strike . . . "

He did not pursue the unpleasant reflection, but pulled a

gun and felt ahead with it before making a move. The voice was nearer now, only a few yards distant, but he could see nothing of the owner.

"Make a good job of it an' the two-fifty is yours. You'll have a clear field when the cows start runnin'—which'll be soon now. Them *hombres* will have suthin' else to occupy 'em."

The eavesdropper stiffened; he knew that voice. Navajo! He could not hear the mumbled reply, but a cracking twig told him that the men were moving—away from him. As silently as speed would permit he retraced his steps, his brain busy with the problem so abruptly presented. Rogue's men were to stampede the herd and something was to be tried. It was not difficult to guess what this was. He hurried to his horse, leapt into the saddle, and raced for the camp.

The sight there draw an oath from his lips. Seated round the cook's fire were Sam Eden, Jeff, and the two women; blanketed forms at the other fire were preparing for their turn of night-riding; they were doomed to have their rest rudely interrupted Jim strode up to the foreman.

"Jeff, I've just got wind of a plot to run off the cows—right now," he cried. "Get busy—no time to talk." He turned to his employer. "You didn't oughta be here, sir," he went on. "You . . . "

An outburst of gun fire and wild yells from over the plain, with the drumming thunder of hoofs cut him short.

"God! they've done it!" he exclaimed.

Stooping swiftly, he seized the seated cattleman by the shoulder and thrust him sideways to the ground. Almost at the same instant, a jet of yellow flame punctured the gloom surrounding the camp and a bullet buried itself in the log against which the invalid had been leaning. Jim's gun barked viciously, twice, and the reports were followed by the breaking of dead wood, as a body falling among the bushes and then—silence.

"Guess I got him," he said quietly. "Saw the glint o' the fire on his gun barrel—just in time."

Though the foreman was at first stunned by the abruptness of the calamity his natural sturdiness soon reasserted itself. The awakened sleepers were sent to the rope corral for mounts, the cattleman, vehemently cursing his helplessness, was lifted back into the wagon, and the women ordered to stay in it also.

Sending the others on, Jeff and Jim turned toward the spot whence the bushwhacker had fired. Sprawling in the undergrowth was the body of a man. Sudden turned it over and struck a match.

"Lasker!" the foreman breathed. "Well, I'm damned."

Both bullets had penetrated his chest and the fellow must have died instantly. Jim was conscious of no regret; he had exterminated a cowardly assassin who was willing to kill for gold; it was a scoundrel less in a land where there were all too many. Leaving the corpse in the bushes, they rode to the bedding ground. Jeff was puzzling over this latest development.

"Lasker, huh? Never did cotton to him, somehow," he mused. "Likely he was planted on us, and mebbe we've bin follered right along." He looked curiously at the man beside him. "How did you get on to it, Jim?"

Jim told of the coyote calls and the fragment of conversation he had overheard, but did not reveal that he recognized one of the voices. He had just finished when a limping figure carrying a saddle, loomed up out of the gloom. It proved to be Sandy.

"You hurt?" Jim asked, observing that Sandy staggered.

"Bullet burned my ribs—nothin' broke," was the reply.

"What happened?" This from the foreman.

"You can search me. First we knowed was the fireworks and the shoutin'—they musta crept up on us.

And believe me, them steers didn't wait to ask questions none whatever. I tried to head 'em off and some jasper started slingin' lead—got my hoss too, blast his soul."

"Which way was the herd travelin'?" Jeff asked.

"West—must be damn near the Pacific Slope by now," was the bitter retort. "Gawd, what a mess!"

"How many of 'em?"

"Couldn't say. It was as dark as the inside of a cow. I only saw the fella who creased me. Fancy I nicked him—heard him cuss."

Sandy assured them he could make camp unaided and the other two rode on. Mile after mile was covered without a trace of the missing herd save the hoofprints which showed they were following at least a portion of it. At length, in the dim, grey light of the dawn, they saw two riders driving a bunch of about a hundred steers. They were less than half a mile distant and not hurrying, apparently deeming themselves safe from pursuit. Jim pulled his rifle from the sheath.

"Hold on, Jim, they may be our fellas," Jeff warned his companion.

"They wouldn't be headed west," Jim pointed out.

"That's so," the foreman admitted, "but I'd rather be sure than sorry. I'll give 'em a hail our boys would reckernize. They can't outrun us with the cows."

His voice rang out in a shrill cowboy call, familiar on many ranges, but with variations Sudden had not heard before. The result dispelled their doubt effectively. The riders' heads jerked round and then their right arms rose and fell as they vigorously plied the quirt. Jim's face was grim as he leveled his weapon.

"Steady, boy," he said to his horse, and pulled the trigger.

They saw the pony on the right stumble and fall, throwing its rider headlong. The other man, with no more than a glance at his companion, spurred his mount furiously and soon left the herd behind. Jim sent an unavailing shot which only served to hurry his movements. A few moments brought them to the fallen man and one look at the oddly twisted, huddled form told them what had happened.

"Broke his neck," Jeff said. "You don't know the gent, I suppose, Jim?"

Jim said no, but it wasn't all the truth, for he had seen the fellow during his sojourn with Rogue.

"Well, let's get after them cows," the foreman said, adding harshly, "This ain't my day for buryin' cattle thieves."

The stolen steers had not run far and the S-E men soon had them rounded up and pointed east again. So they rode in silence for an hour, and then, from the mouth of a shallow arroyo, a horseman emerged and hailed them joyfully:

"Hello Jeff. So you got some too?" It was Dumpy, and as he spoke, his sweaty, dirt-laden features broke into a tired grin of welcome. "Where's the rest of the outfit?"

The foreman raised his shoulders. "You alone?" he asked.

"Jed's in there—" Dumpy pointed to the arroyo—" And say, we got near three hundred cows. She's a dandy place, plenty feed, a pond, and the way in is the only way out."

"See here, Jeff, why not fetch the wagon and camp in the arroyo?" Jim suggested. "Two men could hold the herd in there while the rest of us comb the country."

"You're right, Jim," the foreman agreed. "She's our best bet."

Having driven the cows they had brought through the narrow entrance to the gully, they again rode east, taking Dumpy with them. As they approached the spot where the stampede had taken place the sight of cattle and encircling riders brought a lighter look to Jeff's face.

"We'll make a herd yet, boy," he said.

"Shore we will," Jim rejoined.

All the rest of the outfit were there with the exception of Truthful, of whom no one had any tidings save that he had been with the herd when it began to run. The other men, unable to stay the tide of terrified brutes, contented themselves with following bunches of them and, when the scare died out, driving them back. In this way they had salvaged over four hundred head and a dozen horses.

At the camp itself they found Sandy and Peg-leg sitting by the wagon with rifles. The women were inside with the invalid, who listened silently to his foreman's report.

"We've got around eight hundred and I guess we can search out enough others to go on," Jeff concluded.

The old man glared at him. "Yo're damn right we'll go on," he rasped. "Get this, an' get it straight; I said I'd make this drive and I'll do it, if there's only one blasted cow to take into Kansas."

"That goes with me, and with all of us, I reckon," the foreman said quietly, and went on to tell of Jim's suggestion to move camp.

"Sounds like a good idea," the cattleman agreed. He looked at the cowboy. "Young fella, I figured you saved my life—though I sure thought you'd gone loco. That lead pill went in just where my head had been, and I'm thankin' you. What had Lasker against me, Jeff?"

"We've been framed, Sam; they just waited their chance. Jim got one of 'em."

He related the passing of the unknown rustler and the old man's eyes glowed with savage approval.

six

With the cattle and camp safely hidden in the arroyo, which two men could guard, the remainder of the outfit were free to scour the surrounding country in search of the scattered longhorns. Frequently a steer, having regained its freedom, would fight to retain it, and had to be roped and thrown before it would bow to the inevitable. Despite the difficulties, additions to the herd dribbled in and with each one the foreman's face grew less somber. On the fifth day, however, some of the searchers returned empty-handed, though still nearly half the cattle were missing.

"They musta got away with over a thousand head, reckonin' they'd lose some we ain't found," Jeff said. "We might as well push on; we won't find any more."

"Hold on for another day," Jim advised, "and let me an' Sandy have Jed an' Dumpy tomorrow."

The foreman agreed without question; he was beginning to realize that this cool, capable young cowboy usually had a reason for anything he said or did.

On the following morning the four men set out. Jed, as ever, had his grumble: "Waste o' time. Betcha we don't get a cow apiece."

Sandy grinned at his friend. "Don't tell 'em," he whispered.

"Sure not," Jim said. "Besides, the nest may be empty; the joke would be on us then."

It had been on the first day that the pair of them, returning after a fruitless foray through a broken patch of country some twelves miles from camp, halted abruptly on the edge of a wide swathe of cattle tracks. The fact that the beasts had been bunched together, and the prints of shod horses alongside, told that they had been driven. The S-E men followed the trail to a small, hidden valley, rock-rimmed, the narrow entrance to which was masked by a great boulder and further defended by a rude fence of poles lashed together with rawhide, two of which could be removed to permit passage. Riding through, they found a grass-covered basin in which some hundreds of cows were feeding. There appeared to be no one in charge, and they had no diffuclty in getting near enough to read the brand on the nearest beast.

"S-E," Sandy had cried exultantly. "Jim, our luck has surely changed; here's a gather that'll make Jeff's eyes stick out like they was on stalks. Do we round 'em up?"

Jim shook his head. "Here's how I figure it," he explained. "Rogue's men couldn't hold the herd no more'n we could. They're combin' the country too and bringin' 'em here as they gather 'em. I'm bettin' that if we call again in a few days' time we'll find twice as many."

Sandy let out a whoop. "Jim, yo're a great man," he said. "The notion of lettin' them skunks collect cows for us . . . "

So they had left the valley undisturbed and for the ensuing days had ridden in other directions. It had been a gamble, and they were now on their way to learn if they had lost or won. If the rustlers had removed their plunder . . .

They reached the spot, and leaving Saundy on guard outside, the others rode into the valley. One glance told Jim that he had guessed correctly; the herd had more than doubled; roughly he estimated it at nearly a thousand head, with a sprinkling of horses. His companions yelped gleefully.

"Seems we might git a cow a-piece after all, Jed," the fat man remarked. "Wish I'd took that bet. Why didn't you take him up, Jim?"

"They might not 'a' been here," Jim smiled. "We'll have one fine job handlin' 'em; I didn't expect so many."

"What about sendin' to Jeff for help?" Jed asked.

"Too risky—the rustlers may be showin' up any moment. We'll go while the goin's good. Hell! What's that mean?

Two reports in quick succession shattered the still air and all three men raced for the exit. Fifty yards from the entrance to the valley a man lay sprawling in the sand and Jim's heart skipped a beat. Then he saw that the pony sniffing curiously at the body was not the one Sandy was riding. The man, an evil-faced ruffian whom Sudden did not recognize, had been shot through the throat; his right hand still gripped a heavy revolver, one chamber of which was empty.

"He tried to git Sandy and was got hisself," Jed remarked. "But where in blazes is Sandy?"

Jim had been studying the ground. "Gone after the other," he explained. "Yeah, there was a couple of 'em, and if the second gets clear it's goin' to make things plenty awkward for us." He looked at the brand on the dead man's pony. "That's one of our hosses, and they've fetched us a few more cows."

He pointed to half a dozen longhorns, contentedly grazing a short distance away. A little later, a rider leading a saddle horse topped a nearby ridge of rock and came toward them; it was Sandy. There was no need to ask a question; his pale face and the grim set of his lips told the story. He had killed two men, outlaws, it is true, found with stolen stock in their possession, which in those days meant death; moreover, both had tried to kill him, but nevertheless . . . Jim knew how he was feeling and sent the other men to begin gathering the herd. Sandy supplied the information he would not ask for.

"I had to do it, Jim" he said harshly. "They rode up outa that draw and the fella lyin' there pulled on me without any palaver, and missed. When I downed him, the other bolted. I knowed he'd gotta be stopped. My bronc was better'n his. I could have shot him down from behind but I gave him his chance." He showed the bullet holes in the crown of his hat. "He near got me," he added.

"You done a good job," Jim said sternly. "Know either of 'em?"

"Never seen him afore," Sandy replied, pointing to the man on the ground. "The other was—Ropey."

Jim's mind went back to the outlaw retreat, saw again the dark, sneering face of Navajo when his catspaw had been so completely humiliated. He shrugged his shoulders.

"Well, I ain't mournin'," he said. "C'mon. We've shore got a job of work ahead. We played in luck, Sandy; that herd's doubled since we first saw it." He thought a moment, and added, "What you do with Ropey?"

Sandy looked uncomfortable. "Well, there was a handy hole in the rocks and I—buried him, Jim," he admitted. "You see, I had knowed him—one time."

To his surprise, Jim agreed. "Good idea," he said. "We'll find another niche for this *hombre*.."

Across the back of his own pony, they carried the dead man into a gully, the hard floor of which would leave no telltale hoof marks. Here they found a crevice between two rocks, slid the body in, and piled stones upon it.

"Tough on the buzzards but it can't be helped," Jim said sardonically when they had completed the job. "This'll get Rogue guessin'. When he discovers the herd is gone and these jaspers don't show up he'll think his own men are double-crossin' him. Savvy?"

For the next few hours all four riders were far too busy to think of anything but the work in hand. It was a big bunch for so small a crew, and the cattle—loath to leave the peaceful, sheltered valley, made frequent efforts to break back. By the time the arroyo was reached the men were limp, drenched with perspiration, and utterly profane.

They found the foreman and Carol at the entrance to the arroyo, and the little man's slitted eyes widened when he saw the cattle pouring through.

"Christ-opher Columbus!" he ejaculated, remembering just in time that his employer's daughter was present. "Whose ranch you been raidin', Jim?"

But the girl had seen the brand. "They are our own cows, Jeff," she cried.

Sudden told the tale, omitting, however, the removal of the two rustlers. Jeff swore delightedly to himself as he listened.

"You sure got nerve, boy," he commented. "Lettin' them thieves collect our cows for us was one great scheme."

"Seemed fair to me," Jim smiled. "They scattered 'em."

Jeff's eyes had been busy and as the last of the herd trotted by he slapped his thigh joyously. "Damn near a thousand head," he said. "Why, we won't be more'n three-four hundred shy after all!"

"We'll be all fixed to take the trail in the morning'," Jeff went on. Jim's eye brows rose and he shot a whimsical glance at the sun overhead. The foreman read it. "Yo're thinkin' we oughta start now?" he asked.

"Think it over," the cowboy replied. "We don't know how soon them *hombres* will discover their loss, but you can bet they won't waste no time high-tailin' it after us—follerin' the cattle won't be no trick at all, we couldn't blind our tracks. Any lead we can get will be all to the good."

"You're damn right," Jeff agreed. "We want to be

plenty absent when they arrive. Sandy, go tell the boys we'll be settin' out *pronto.*"

When they were alone, Jim told of the dead rustlers—concealing the fact that they recognized one of them—and concluding his recital with, "Sandy ain't advertisin' it."

"Natural enough, though some fellas wouldn't talk of nothin' else," the foreman said. "That was a cute move to hide the remainders, Jim," he continued, admiration in his smiling eyes. "You don't overlook many bets, do you?"

In less than an hour the herd was again on the move, heading away from where they conjectured the rustlers to be encamped. Despite the disaster, cheerfulness reigned. The loss had proved far less than had seemed likely, and the riders, with the optimism born of their hardy natures, had already transformed the incident into a victory; they had "put one over" the cattle thieves.

Jim reined in his horse on the top of a broken-backed ridge and surveyed the surrounding scenery; the indentation between his level brows denoted that he was not entirely pleased with what he saw. Since the stampede and the events which followed it, day after day passed in wearying but satisfactory monotony.

For the last day or so Jim had been wondering whether, in their search for easy going, they had veered too much to the west. Now, it was clear that the surface of the prairie was changing, the grass was becoming sparse and sand was taking its place. Ahead of him, a giant cactus, its candelabra-like arms curving upward, stood like a warning sentinel. Far away, almost on the horizon, a swarm of black dots moved slowly nearer. He rode back to the herd.

"Desert ahead," he said briefly. "Ain't drifted onto the Stake Plain, have we?"

The question put a perturbed expression on the foreman's lined features. *Llano Estacado,* or the Staked Plain, so-called from that early day when posts with buffalo skulls atop to guide those who might follow, had an evil reputation. A desolate and sterile tableland, without water or timber, its scant vegetation consisting of sage, greasewood, mesquite and cactus. Well might a cattleman shudder at the prospect of taking a herd over that trackless waste of sand.

"Hell, Jim, I can't say," Jeff confessed. "That cussed stampede throwed us right out, and I dunno nothin' about this blame' country. Mebbe we're only on the fringe of it."

"Better swing to the east anyway," Jim advised. "There's a herd of buffalo a-comin' and if our cows get mixed up with it . . . "

"Shore they ain't hosses?" he asked anxiously.

"No, it's buffalo, an' likely there's redskins not far off," the cowboy replied.

Jeff gave the necessary instruction to the point men and then rode ahead with Jim.

They were satisfied that they could do so safely, they rode after the herd. Jeff bit on an oath; the cattle were floundering through a sea of sand, hummocks, ridges and long rolling swells stretched out unendingly until they merged with the pale blue of the cloudless sky.

Mile upon mile under the pitiless sun they crawled, both men and beasts choking in the cloud of dust churned up by thousands of tramping feet. On all sides lay the arid waste of bleached sand.

The cool night air brought some slight mitigation of their sufferings, but instead of being baked they were nearly frozen. At the first glimmer of grey in the east they arose, shivering, swallowed a scanty breakfast, and set out; the foreman was anxious to get as far as possible before the sun's rays attained their full force. The day proved to be a repetition of the preceding, the discomfort intensified by the fact that even the miserable ration of water they had then enjoyed was no longer available; a quart or so, reserved for the invalid and the women, was all that remained. The soft sand, clinging to their feet, made every step an effort. The cowboys, slouched in their saddles, and croaked weird curses beneath the handkerchiefs which covered the lower part of their faces.

By mid-day it was evident the cows could not go much farther. Already a few had fallen and had to be abandoned; the rest still staggered weakly on, tongues protruding, sullenly lowing, and many of them nearly blind. The foreman ranged up beside Jim, who was leading the herd. His voice was little more than a whisper:

"Jim, if we don't git outa this Devil's oven mighty soon it's our finish. That black of yores appears to be in better shape than any of the hosses; ride on and take a look-see."

Jim nodded and forged ahead. He had covered about a mile when a flat hummock of rock attracted his attention and he rode to the top of it. From there he had a more extended view. Wiping the bitter alkali dust from his smarting eyes he stared unbelievingly. Was it a mirage, that maddening mockery of the desert, or did he really see a dark, irregular line between the sky and sand? He gazed again, intently, but the vision persisted. He tried to utter a whoop, but his swollen tongue and parched throat produced only a hoarse crackle. When the herd came in sight, a straggling string of grey ghosts, he waved an arm and Jeff joined him. The foreman's squinting eyes followed the pointing finger, and he managed to articulate:

"If them's trees, it means runnin' water. Ride on, Jim, there may be Injuns about."

Jim departed, taking his own and Jeff's empty canteens. Gradually, as he approached it, the dark line thickened and presently took the form of foliage. At the same time, the sand was disappearing, tussocks of grass, clumps of cactus, dwarfed mesquite and sage taking its place. In a few moments they saw the river, a sluggish stream less than a hundred yards across, passing between wide sloping banks. Sudden drank sparingly, dipped his head in the water, and then dragged his unwilling mount from it.

At the top of the bank, Jim mounted and rode back to carry the good news. The foreman's face brightened, and when he had moistened his aching throat and sent the canteens back down the line, he looked at the stumbling beasts beside him, and said:

"They'll just about make it—we'll lose some, mebbe, but that can't be helped. They's perkin' up already. See ol' Show-'em-how there; he can smell that damn water."

At the head of the herd the big longhorn was striding gallantly along, nose up, nostrils distended, and from time to time he gave vent to a feeble bellow, as of a leader encouraging his followers.

"We'll have to rest 'em for a day or so," the foreman continued. "She ain't much of a river, you say?"

"That's so, but I'd rest 'em on the other side," Jim advised. "She's low now, but come a storm, she'd be a rip-roaring devil. Get 'em over, *pronto,* old-timer."

"Any special reason for sayin' that, Jim?" Jeff inquired. "Them steers is plenty tuckered out for swimmin'."

"There ain't much of that and they'll feel different after a swim," Jim told him. "See here, Jeff; the water is risin'—only by inches—but that means more to come."

The other nodded agreement; he knew how quickly a stream showing a mere trickle of water could become a raging torrent. They had almost reached the river when Jim's restless eyes lighted on the remains of a fire, almost hidden behind a big cactus. They rode to the spot.

"Injuns?" the foreman inquired, indicating a mocassin track.

Jim shook his head. "The sticks is laid criss-cross and burned in the middle, white man fashion; a redskin lays 'em all pointin' to the center and burns the ends." He searched the surrounding ground. "Ain't no hoofprints. What's a white man on foot doin' in these parts?"

"I got riddles enough already," Jeff said drily. "Best get that cussed wagon an' hosses over first, I suppose."

So the herd was held back till this was done. Fortunately the bed of the stream was firm, and—as Jim had guessed—there was not, as yet, much deep water, so the unwieldly vehicle was transported without undue difficulty. The remuda followed, and then came the cattle. Tumbling pell-mell down the bank, the parched brutes staggered into the water and stood there as though rooted.

"G'wan, you can drink and swim one time," Dumpy yelled, jabbing a spear into obstinate ribs.

But even the pitiless application of quirts and rope ends failed to stir the stubborn steers, and the foreman scratched his head in perplexity. It was Jim who saw the solution.

"Keep on pilin' em in, Jeff," he cried.

The plan worked. The pressure of the thirsty ones behind forced the leaders into deep water and soon they were swimming for the other bank. The foreman breathed again, but his troubles were not yet at an end. The crossing was only nearing completion when a warning came from Sandy:

"Hurry 'em up, Jeff; she's risin' rapid."

It was true; the span of the river was twice what it had been, and the outfit, recognizing the danger, made desperate efforts to hustle over the rest of the herd. Sluggishly, as it seemed, the jaded longhorns fought their way through the deepening water and climbed the opposing slope, reluctant to leave the liquid they had for forty-eight hours been without.

"We'll make it," Jeff said, relief in his tone.

He spoke too soon. The last of the "drag"—consisting of the weaker animals in the charge of Jed, was little more than halfway across when a dull, booming sound which grew louder every moment sent all eyes up-stream, There the banks rose steeply, they saw a sight to make the bravest quail. Piled up between the bluffs was a great wall of water twenty feet high, the foaming crest lip of which bristled with driftwood, great branches and even whole trees, torn up bodily by the torrent.

The cowboy saw the danger, and leaving his charges to fend for themselves, spurred his mount in an endeavor to reach the bank. But the peril was advancing too swiftly. With a thunderous crash the avalanche of water broke upon the struggling forms and swept them from sight. Cursing in their helplessness, the rest of the outfit watched their comrade go to his doom. All except Jim, who, at the first glimpse of the threatening deluge, had raced his horse to a jutting point in the bank and, at the risk of being swept away himself, had swung his rope. The loop dropped over Jed's shoulders just as the limb of a tree struck him from his saddle and buried him in a seething welter of tormented water.

Feeling that the rope, already tied to the horn, was taut, Jim backed his horse slowly away from the river. A cheer greeted him when it was seen that the limp figure of the cowboy was at the end of the lariat. Willing hands carried him to a dry spot and sought for injuries; beyond a scratch or two, there was none. Dumpy, who with a strangely pale face, had been feeling anxiously for broken bones, gasped with relief when the rescued man suddenly opened his eyes and sat up.

"So you ain't drowned?" he said fatuously.

"Course I am, you chump," Jed retorted. "My insides is, anyway. Damn this country, there ain't no reasonableness in it; you either gets too much or none at all of most things. You needn't look so glad I ain't gone neither."

seven

The days that followed seemed like a dream after the rude experience of the desert. The character of the country had changed; there were still stretches of grass-covered prairie but they were not so extensive, and varied by hills and dales, some of them thickly wooded. Creeks were frequent, and with abundant feed and water, the cattle quickly recovered. Beyond the certainty that they were still in Indian territory and were heading north, they had no knowledge of their position.

"We've shook off Mister Rogue," Sandy remarked to Jim.

"Rogue knows where we're makin' for—he don't have to follow us. What's worryin' me is not seein' any Injuns."

"Well, that's a misfortune I can bear easy," Sandy said. "Mebbe we've just been lucky."

Jim declined to accept this view. "I've a hunch we're bein' watched," he said.

"You've been rubbin' noses with Jed," Sandy chaffed. "The war-whoops is all busy chasin' the festive buffalo."

Jim started to grin, changed his mind, and gripped a gun instead. "Here's some that ain't," he said quietly.

Out of the brush a line of horsemen had silently emerged, pulling up in the form of a half-circle about two hundred yards from the herd. They were Indians, sitting their mettlesome little ponies like bronze statues.

At the sight of them the cowboys pulled out their rifles,

but the Indians showed no hostility. Only one advanced, a tall oldish man, gaily bedecked with eagle plumes. His right hand was raised, palm outwards, in token that he came on a peaceful mission. He rode straight to the foreman—having doubtless observed him giving orders—uttered a guttural "How!" and began to speak. Jeff listened for a moment and shook his head.

"No savvy," he said, and beckoned to Jim.

"Mebbe you can find out what he's after."

The redskin repeated his statement and the cowboy was able to gather the gist of it.

"He says he is Black Bear, a great chief, that this is Comanche country, and we got no right to take cattle through it," he translated. "He wants tribute in cows." The foreman's face grew bleak. "How many?" he asked.

Sudden put the question and the Indian, resting his lance across his knees, pointed first to himself, then to Jim and raised both hands.

Jim explained, "Redskins reckon this-away; one is a finger, five a hand, ten, two hands, twenty, a man. You can figure it yourself."

Jeff, who had been watching the chief's movements closely, did so and swore. "Give him fifty steers?" he snarled. "Tell him to go to hell."

"Don't know enough of the lingo," Jim said. "I'll offer him five."

Black Bear listened gravely to the white man's explanation, haltingly told in a mixture of Indian tongues, and ending with the raising of one hand only. Then he drew himself up haughtily, flashed a meaning glance at his followers, and fixed his savage eyes on this paleface who had insulted him with so paltry an offer. Jim met the stare with one equally steady. For one long moment the black eyes battled with the blue and then the redskin wrenched his pony round and trotted back to his band. The cowboys, who had allowed the herd to drift toward the other end of the valley, waited, rifles ready, for the expected charge. They saw Black Bear rejoin his men and face about but he gave no signal.

"What's the game, Jim?" the foreman asked, anxiously scanning the line of silent savages.

"Damned if I know," Jim replied. "Looks like they're waitin' for somethin'."

The crash of a gun, followed by the fainter report of a pistol, came from where the camp lay and instantly a rider whirled his mount and spurred in that direction; it was Sandy. The Indians were gesticulating, waving their weapons, and reining in their ponies. Jim turned to the foreman.

"They're attackin' the camp—that's why these devils were holdin' back. I'll follow Sandy; you can handle this bunch."

A pressure of his knees and he was off, threading his way through the scared cattle. He had covered but a short distance when a burst of yells, mingled with the spiteful crack of exploding powder, told him that the enemy had charged.

Sandy reached the camping ground just in time to see a tall, lithe warrior, with a limp form draped over his shoulder, disappear in the brush, and oblivious to everything else, dashed in pursuit. He knew that his friend was just behind him, for he had seen the big black pounding down the valley. The trees hampered him and he arrived in the open only to see the abductor sling his burden like a sack of meal across the back of a waiting pony, spring up behind it, and dart away. The cowboy dared not risk a shot lest he hit the girl; he could but try to run the redskin down.

Jim arrived on the heels of Sandy, saw him vanish, and turned his attention to what was happening. A dead Indian—his head half blown away—sprawled in his path, and another lay huddled by the wagon, from which a steady string of curses issued. Near the fire, Peg-leg was outstretched, a smear of blood on his face, and over his body Aunt Judy was struggling desperately with a squat, bow-legged savage, whose hideously-painted features she had further decorated with several vivid red streaks. Fighting like a wildcat, and spitting oaths of which a cow-boy might well have been proud, she was giving the Comanche brave plenty to think about. Try as he might, he could not clutch those long bony arms with their fearsome claws.

"Knock my man over, huh, ye Gawd-damned, mis-begotten, copper-colored heathen," she yelled, and with a quick stoop, snatched a skillet from the fire and whanged him across the face.

Driven back by the blow, the redskin drew his knife. His hand swung up and then a bullet from Jim's gun toppled him to the ground. Aunt Judy staggered weakly to her husband, flinging herself on her knees beside him. As she wiped away the blood, the cook opened his eyes and sat up.

"I'm awright," he said. "One of them got me with the butt of his lance and I took the count." His eyes roamed round the little clearing. "There was four of 'em. Where's the other?"

"Got away, takin' Miss Carol," Aunt Judy told him.

Jim interrupted by putting a question. It appeared the raiders had approached the camp on foot. Peg-leg had seen one stepping to the wagon and laid him out with a shotgun. Then he had been struck down from behind. His wife took up the tale. The women had been in the tent and when Peg-leg fired, the girl ran out, to be immediately seized, overpowered, and tied. Aunt Judy following, was attacked by a third savage, while a fourth attempted to climb into the wagon.

"Sam blowed his light out and he's liable to do the same to us if he ain't attended to," she finished.

They found the cattleman propped up on one elbow, a

six-shooter gripped in his right hand. The fury in his rugged face gave way to fear when he heard of Carol's capture, and he cursed and anew the man whose bullet had laid him low. Jim tried to soothe him by pointing out that Sandy was in pursuit, but the effort failed.

"They'll get him too—damn the crooked luck," he dejectedly replied. "How's Jeff makin' it?"

Hammering hoofs brought the answer and the Infant pulled his panting pony to a sliding stop by the wagon.

"We drove 'em off," he announced triumphantly. "Got six at the first rattle. That discouraged 'em some, and they started circlin'. It didn't help 'em none, for we got two-three more. Then the ol' chief lets out a whoop an' they scoops up their dead an' vanishes—complete. Jeff said for to tell you the herd ain't scattered much an' we'll be ready to start in 'bout an hour."

Jim explained why this would not be possible and the youth's face lengthened.

"Hell, that's bad," he said. "Sandy went after her?"

"Yeah, an' as he ain't back, it's possible they got him too."

The rancher's querulous voice came from the wagon: "Get Jeff an' the boys an' go after these damned women-stealers."

Jim shook his head. "Listen to me." he said earnestly. "That Black Bear is a wise *hombre* and he'll figure on us doin' that very thing, which is why he didn't stay and fight it out; Comanches ain't cowards, you savvy. If they can trap the outfit they get the herd easy."

"To hell with the herd," Eden snapped. "I'd sooner lose every hoof than harm should happen to Carol."

"Sure, but that ain't the way to go about it," Jim said. "We gotta walk in the water some."

"He's right, boss," Peg-leg put in. "Let Jim trail 'em and see how things is. No sense in runnin' our heads into a yeller-jacket's nest."

The old man gave a grudging assent; he knew they were advising him wisely.

Jim's preparations were soon made. He decided to take the black, for if he could liberate the captives, speed would be essential. He was mounting when Jeff rode in; Jim explained his errand.

"Of course, it's in the cards they'll gather me in too," he said. "Then it'll be up to you an' the boys. I'll leave a plain trail."

The foreman's face was somber. "It looks bad, Jim," he said. "Them skunks was on'y there to keep the boys busy while the others raided the camp. Why should they be so set on gettin' a white woman, huh?"

Sudden did not reply to the question. He could have offered a reason but he feared the foreman would deem it fantastic. But his knowledge of redskin nature, relentless and untiring in its pursuit of vengeance, told him that it was possible. All he said was:

"Well, they paid a price. So long, old timer. See you soon—mebbe."

Following Sandy's trail, his mind was busy with idea he had forborne to mention to the foreman. It had suggested itself when he learned the girl had been carried off. The braves from whom he had rescued her on the day he had first ridden to the S-E had been Comanches, and there was a chance that they belonged to Black Bear's tribe. In any case, they were chiefs, men of importance. Had the one who escaped remained in the neighborhood, watching the preparations for the drive, following it day by day, waiting for the opportunity to avenge his comrade? Jim's thoughts reverted to the moccasin prints he had found when Eden was stricken down. No Indian had fired that shot, but one might have been spying on the camp and driven away by the advent of the assassin. If this theory were correct, the girl's peril was indeed dire.

He experienced no difficulty in following the trail since

neither pursuer nor pursued had any other thought than speed. The deeper indentations of the animal carrying the double burden could be distinguished.

At a point where the foliage overhead made the wood almost dark, he came upon evidences that a struggle had taken place; the carpet of pine needles had been violently disturbed, and on the bole of a tree was a spot of blood. Had Sandy caught his man? Jim did not think so—the indications suggested that it was the other way about. A careful examination of the nearby tree trunks showed that the ground behind several was slightly flattened. Moreover, the trail of the two horses continued on through the wood.

"That *hombre* had it all planned out," Jim muttered. "They were waitin' here for a pursuin' party. Well, Sandy ain't dead, seemingly, or they'd have scalped and left him."

"Somewhat cheered by this reflection, he rode on, noting that the bloodstains recurred at intervals. Presently he emerged from the timber and at once pulled up; an increase in the hoofprints showed that other riders had joined the pair he was following.

"The ambushin' braves picked up their hosses about here," he surmised. "Must be near a dozen of 'em. Now we gotta watch out."

He went on cautiously. But he had to take some risks, for the day was advancing and it would be hopeless to follow the trail in the dark. A little later he came to a narrow ravine littered with boulders, debris wrested by the weather from the rock walls. Pacing slowly along, eyes alert for any sound or movement, he saw something which brought an oath to his lips. Lying face downward at the side of the gully was a bound and gagged man. Jim slid from his saddle and turned him over; it was Sandy. As he stooped to remove the gag, a rope swished, he was flung violently backwards, and a savage war cry peeled out.

Realizing that he, too, had been tricked, he grabbed at a gun but a crashing blow from behind knocked him out.

When he regained his senses he was lying on his back, hands tied and unable to find out the extent of his injury. In the semi-darkness he could see that he was inside an Indian wigwam.

"So they got me," he said aloud. "If my head didn't hurt so much I'd say it was solid bone. Wonder where Sandy is?"

"Hello, Jim," a low voice answered. "You come to life again?"

"No, I'm dead from the neck up," was the disgusted reply. "Of all the fools . . . "

"It was neat, allasame," Sandy consoled. "They knowed you'd hop off to tend to me—any fella would. All they had to do was squat behind the rocks and rope you. First time I ever figured as the bait in a trap."

"Where's Miss Carol?"

"Right here, wore out and sleepin'. What d'you reckon they'll do to us, Jim?"

"Cuff our ears and tell us to be good boys in the future, don't you reckon?" was his sarcastic reply, and then, "Shucks, we'll find a way out." After a pause, "There was blood on the trail; you hurt?"

"No, I winged one when they jumped me," Sandy explained.

"Jeff and the boys'll search us out," Jim said.

"Don't bet on it. Soon after they collected you the main bunch branched off, takin' your hoss and mine. One brave reckoned on ridin' the black but that pet of yores just planted both hind hoofs on his chest. After that, they elected to lead him. Well, the rest of us struck a stream, waded down it for near half a mile, and then went along a stony gulch where a herd o' buffalo wouldn't leave a trace."

Jim was silent; this put a different complexion on matters. The rescue party would follow the prints of the shod horses and probably blunder into a trap just as he and Sandy had done.

There was a slight movement in the gloom on the far side of the wigwam; the third prisoner had awakened.

"Sandy," the girl whispered. "Did I hear Mister Green's voice?"

"Sure, I'm here, Miss Carol," Jim said.

"Thank heaven," she said. "I feared you were—killed." He smiled grimly into the darkness; she did not realize that death might yet be a boon to crave for. Still speaking in a low voice, she went on, "Mister Green, the Indian who brought me here is the other—the one who got away."

It gave Jim no pleasure to find that his conjecture had proven correct. Affecting a jocularity he did not feel, he said:

"Perservering beggar; we'll have to discourage him some."

"I'm scared," she confessed.

"Don't you be," he urged, and then lied nobly, "the boys'll be along any time now and snake us outa this mess."

The flap of the tent was flung aside and a savage, carrying a lighted pine knot, stalked in. He shot one triumphant glance at the girl, strode across to Jim and stooped, thrusting the torch almost into the cowboy's face. For an instant he gazed and then a flash of ferocious joy lit up the dark eyes.

Spitting out a few rapid sentences in his own tongue, the Indian, after testing the bonds of all three, went away.

"What did he say?" Sandy thoughtlessly inquired.

Jim, though he could not have given a literal translation, gathered sufficient to know that he had been promised a slow and very agonizing end. Not wishing to further alarm the girl, his reply was evasive:

"He's goin' to have a pow-wow with me in the mornin'."

Daylight brought them visitors, an armed brave and a squaw bearing platters of food, pieces of cooked flesh and cakes of meal, with which they had to deal as best they would with bound hands. One unacquainted with Indians might have argued from this that they were not yet to die, but Jim knew it was but a refinement of curelty; a man weak from want of food would succumb to torture sooner.

When they had eaten, the redskin removed the bonds from Jim's ankles and pointed to the entrance of the tent. The cowboy saw the alarm in the girl's eyes and forced a grin on his set lips.

"Goin' to have a word with Foxy," he said. "Back soon."

"What does it really mean?" Carol's white lips whispered, as the pair went out.

Sandy was cursing softly but vividly. "It means—hell," he groaned.

They heard a fierce yell of execration as the captive appeared, and in an agony of fear, dragged themselves to the opening of the wigwam. The sight they saw did not reassure them.

The camp was of fair size, consisting of more than a score of tents, set in a rude circle, and hedged in by trees and brush. Round the open space in the cneter the whole tribe was gathered, men, women, and children, shrieking and yelling. The hubbub increased as the white man was conducted to a large tree on the edge of the clearing. Two more warriors now joined the first. Releasing his hands, they gripped a wrist apiece, forced his arms back and again secured them behind the tree trunk. The position was intensely painful and rendered the sufferer as helpless as a tied steer.

No sooner was this done than the onlookers surged forward, broke into an eerie chant, and began to circle the tree in a wild dance. Though they shook their weapons in his face, not one of the dancers attempted to touch the prisoner. Interminably, as it seemed to the object of it, the monotonous dirge went on. All the tribe were not taking part; on the far side of the clearing stood a group of Indians whose plumed heads showed that they were chiefs; among them was Black Bear.

Wooden-faced, the bound man stared stolidly at the dancing devils who mocked as they passed him. His head still throbbed from the rough treatment of yesterday and his arm muscles ached under the unnatural strain to which they were being subjected, but he knew he must show no sign of weakness. It would be Sandy's turn next, and then the girl; the eyes of Red Fox had plainly told her fate.

A raucous command rang out and the droning ring broke and swept back, forming in a half-circle on the far side of the clearing. From among the chiefs Red Fox strode, his feathers fluttering in the faint breeze, to pause a few paces from the prisoner. His dark face was alight with savage triumph.

"Paleface dog!" he hissed.

"For the slaying of Running Deer, my brother, you shall die many times," the chief went on, and the cowboy knew the reason for the long delay and carefully prepared vengeance. "On your knees and shall beg for death and it shall not come."

Jim's expression was contemptuous. "Red Fox has a big mouth," he said. "He might frighten a papoose."

He knew that the shaft had gone home, though only a tremor of rage betrayed the fact; the redskin was crafty.

"Red Fox has sharp teeth but will not bite too soon," he countered. "Yet if the white dog desires a speedy death, he shall have his chance."

He stepped back, drew a short, heavy-shafted knife from his belt, and glanced pridefully round at his audience. Then his right arm swung up, down, and like a streak of silver the blade flashed through the sunlight and embedded itself in the tree trunk. Jim felt a trickle of warm blood and realized that the keen edge, missing his head by a hair's breadth, had nicked his ear. The thrower, bent slightly forward, watched the result of his effort with evil enjoyment.

"Move, and earn the death you will presently pray for," he called out.

A medley of mocking yells came from the spectators and a score of voices repeated the taunt; they and the cunning devil who had uttered it knew that the invitation could not be accepted. However desperate his situation, a sane, healthy man will hold on to life as long as possible, and though Jim could see no chance of escape, he cherished a hope that he might somehow get free and go down dighting. So he schooled his aching muscles and became as motionless as the tree against which he stood.

With steady, unwinking eyes, he saw the fling of the brown arm again, the gleam of the twinkling steel, and felt the wind of the blade on his cheek. The second knife missed him by less than an inch. Amid the shouts of admiration for the prowess of their chief, were jeers for the man who had declined to die. Jim was concerned with something else; from behind had come a hoarse whisper:

"Your han's is free. When that varmint comes to git his stickers, grab one and let him have it. Then jump for the tepee, git your guns, and gimme a chance to start the gal and your friend off. There'll be a hoss waitin' for you."

Like a dazed man, the cowboy listened. The voice was one he had heard before but in the stress of the moment he could not place it. He could feel that his wrists had been loosed, and lowered his arms slightly to relieve the numbing ache. He looked at Red Fox; the chief was strutting to and fro, enjoying his triumph, and seemed to be in no hurry to getch his weapons. Jim wanted him nearer.

"Red Fox is clumsy," he announced loudly. "An

Apache or Kiowa boy could throw the knife better."

Like a stung man the savage whirled, his features aflame with fury.

"White spawn!" he cried. "I will cut off your ears with the knives; I will pin your fingers one by one to the tree."

He stepped forward and that was the moment the victim had been waiting for. Snatching one of the knives, he balanced it on his palm for an instant, and then hurled it at the advancing savage. With a strangled cry Red Fox crumpled up, the steel buried to the haft in his throat.

For one staggering moment there was silence and then the petrified onlookers saw the man they had believed to be securely tied leap across the open space and vanish into one of the wigwams. The sight restored their power to move and with a ferocious threatening howl, they rushed in pursuit.

Jim found the tent empty. Buckling on his belt, he drew both guns and sprang to the entrance. A surging wave of maddened redskins was sweeping down upon him, and a cloud of arrows greeted his appearance, piercing the buffalo hide walls of the wigwam, and whistling past his ears. His Colts spouted flame and before that continuous hail of hurtling lead the charge withered and broke, the Indians scattering in all directions. But he knew the respite was but momentary; they would surround him, and then . . . Reloading his weapons, he became aware that someone had entered, and swung about. He saw a brown-paint-smeared face, feathered scalplock, and his thumb was on the point of releasing the hammer when the intruder spoke:

"Hold on there, friend; I ain't no war-whoop."

It was the voice of the man who had freed him, and now he remembered it as that of the "Still-hunter" who had come into their camp on the Colorado. Tyson gave him no time for questions.

"The gal is away on your black and your friend with her, though he balked some at leavin' you," he said. "There's a hoss waitin' and you ain't got but a minute—them devils is closin' in, which is why they've stopped yappin'." He pointed to the back of the wigwam, where a long slit in the hide covering provided an exit, adding, "It'll be nip an' tuck as it is."

"What about you?" the cowboy asked.

"I'm stayin'," was the jaunty reply. "I can pass as one of 'em."

Sudden did not attempt to dissuade him; Tyson evidently knew what he was about. He held out a hand.

"This puts me deep in your debt," he said.

"Not a bit—I ain't forgot that grub and smokin'," was the reply. "Head due west."

Jim slid through the opening and found the horse. Being Indian property there was no saddle, but the hackamore bridle was all the cowboy needed and in a trice he was on the beast's back and spurring for the open. A shout of rage and a few spasmodic arrows greeted his appearance and a redskin rose out of the long grass and sprang at him, only to go down with a shriek under the plunging feet. A score of leaping strides and the fugitive knew that he was safe for the time. He would be pursued, but the Indians had first to secure their ponies and this would give him a fair start. Nevertheless, he pressed on at full speed, casting an occasional glance at the trail, where the prints of shod horses seemed to indicate that he was following his friends.

Jim had covered but a few miles when, from the crest of a long slope, he saw the pair he was in search of, and uttered a man-sized curse when he realized that they were waiting for him. With a violent gesture he signed them to go on and let his own mount feel the spurs. His greeting, when he ranged alongside, was hardly one of gratitude.

"Have you lost your wits?" he asked Sandy. "You oughta be a couple miles further away right now."

"We were anxious about you," the girl explained. "I insisted on waiting."

Jim looked around disgustedly. "There ain't a hole we could hide in," he said.

As they surmounted another incline a faint whoop was borne to them on the breeze, and back on the trail was a billowing cloud of dust in which tiny dark forms could be dimly distinguished. Jim's lips clamped together as he studied the animal he bestrode. Sandy was riding his own horse, which was a good one.

"Friend Tyson don't savvy ponies, or mebbe this is all he could lay his paws on," he commented. He reached over and removed his rifle from the saddle of the black, and said to Sandy. "You and Miss Carol go ahead; my hoss is fast for a mile or two, but ain't got no bottom."

"Like hell we will," Sandy said. "What you goin' to do?"

"Stay and argue with these copper-colored gents. That'll give you time to get the girl away—mebbe."

Before Sandy could voice his objection to this proposal a fierce yell apprised them of another factor to be considered, and effectually closed the argument. Less than half a mile distant, and coming towards them, was another band of redskins who, at the sight of the whites, quirted their ponies into a run. The fugitives were between two fires. Jim swung his horse to the right. "Follow me," he cried. "We gotta find a better place than this to stand 'em off."

"Mebbe they'll scrap with each other and give us a chance to sneak off," Sandy said hopefully, as they raced at top speed across the plain.

"The second lot are Comanches too," Jim said, and shot a hasty glance over his shoulder. "Hell, they're gainin'. Head for that bluff; it looks a likely spot."

He pointed to a small plateau, the approaching slope of which was, at one spot, broken away, leaving a vertical wall. At the foot of this were several boulders. With the girl and the horses sheltered behind the largest of these, the two men gripped their weapons and waited. They knew their case was desperate, that they had scarcely one chance in a hundred, but death itself was preferable to falling into the hands of the foe again.

"They may get us, boy, but we'll make 'em pay," Jim grated.

eight

The onslaught did not come at once. The white men saw the two bands meet and fraternize, with much shouting, gesticulation, and brandishing of weapons. Probably the position their prey had taken up did not please them; it meant a frontal attack, and most Indians had a healthy fear of the "guns that fired forever." Sandy was counting.

"Thirty of 'em," he said in a low voice. "If they wait till dark we ain't got a hope."

"They won't—Injuns don't like nightwork—too many bad spirits about," Jim reminded him. "They may decide to sit down and starve us out."

Sandy's face lengthened; they had neither food nor water. Lying, each behind a sheltering rock, they awaited the outcome of the argument taking place amongst the enemy.

"Odd that fella Tyson showin' up," Sandy remarked. "He busted in on us just as you hid the knife in that skunk's gullet, and believe me, he was welcome. Hell! they're goin'."

The savages, strung out in a long line, had turned tail and were trotting slowly away.

"No such luck," Jim said. "They're a-comin'. Don't shoot till you're sure and aim low; if you miss the man you'll get the hoss."

He was right; with a whoop the warriors whirled their ponies and raced at the men they had hoped to catch unprepared. Like an incoming wave they swept on and it seemed inevitable that the white men must be overwhelmed. Jim waited until they were some fifty paces distant, and then:

"Let 'em have it," he said.

The reports of the repeating rifles rang out and gaps showed in the advancing line as men and horses went down. Not waiting to reload, the defenders drew their pistols—which at the short range were as effective—and continued the fusillade. The deadly stream of lead was too much for the attackers; the line broke in the middle, the two halves sweeping round, to retreat at full speed. A grin spread over Sandy's perspiring features.

"Reckon they won't come that caper again," he said, busy recharging his weapon. "Funny thing they didn't use their bows."

"Want us alive," Sudden explained. "I'm bettin' they didn't savvy we'd get our guns."

"Well, they know now," Sandy said, "though there's some it won't interest no more."

He nodded grimly at the plain before them, where the bodies of seven men and as many horses could be seen. Even as they looked, one of the former rose, and crouching, ran rowards his friends. Sandy's rifle cracked and the runner reeled and fell.

"Been watchin' that jasper," the marksman said callously. "Had a notion I only got his bronc. Hi, Jim, they're linin' up; looks like they aim to have another try."

The long line was moving forward again but this time it extended farther—yards separating the riders. Also, they were moving slowly, the ponies gradually gathering pace for the final dash. This made the task of the defenders more difficult, for instead of firing into a mass, they had to place every shot.

"No use waitin' till they're near," Jim said. "Pick your man and let fly soon as he's in range."

"I'm takin' that jigger on the pinto," Sandy said, and pulled the trigger. "Cuss the luck," he added, as the horse went down, and its rider, after rolling on the ground, arose and shook a vengeful fist.

Sudden toppled a tall warrior from his seat and then an amazing change came over the scene. From somewhere behind the attacking line rang out a volley of rifle-fire which send half a dozen ponies careening masterless across the plain. The Comanches, taken utterly by surprise, scattered and fled, hotly pursued by the newcomers, who wore the garb of white men. Sandy swung his hat and whooped.

"It'll be the boys, Jim; they've found us at last," he cried. "Why you lookin' as if you'd lost a dollar?"

"If that's the outfit, the S-E has been takin' on hands—there was a dozen of 'em," Jim replied. "Ever hear of the famous steak that fell outa the frying pan?"

Before Sandy could reply, the rescuers came racing back, and their leader, reining in, pushed up the brim of his battered sombrero and disclosed the malevolent face of Navajo. He grined evilly as he recognized the men to whose aid he had come.

"Well, well, see who's here," he drawled. "Sandy, his sidekick, an' "—his triumphant eyes traveled to the girl—"that must be Eden's gal. Sure was lucky for you that we took a fancy to see what mischief this red scum was up to."

"We're obliged to you," Sudden said shortly.

"Oh, yeah," Navajo sneered. "But seein' we're Rogue's men you'll have to thank him in person. I'm bettin' he'll be pleased to see you."

"I was wantin' a word with Rogue anyway," Jim said.

"Good, then we'll be movin'—I reckon them 'paints has got their needlin's," Navajo returned. His eyes narrowed. "There's only one point: you boys must be tired; guess we'll carry your guns for you."

Jim laughed scornfully. "You don't guess very good," he retorted. "If you want our weapons you'll have to buy 'em and the price will be high. *Sabe?*"

Navajo did. The cowboy rested his rifle against a rock and now stood with hands hovering over the butts of his revolvers, his slitted eyes boring into those of the other. The half-breed hesitated; he had seen those long, nervous fingers at work before. It was twelve against two, but . . . His glance went to the plain, still dotted with brown bodies. His shoulders shrugged submission.

"You and your men lead the way—we'll follow," Jim said. "At the first sign of funny business, you'll take a header into hell, Navajo."

The man scowled, but made no reply. He realized that the prisoners would be of no use dead, and he was not sure of his leader's attitude toward them; Rogue did not confide in him. So, when they set out, he and his men went first, followed by Jim and Sandy with the girl riding between them. Carol, who had not heard all that passed, was curious.

"Who are these men?" she asked.

"Some of Rogue's Riders an' they are takin' us to their chief," Jim told her. "We ain't out o' the woods yet."

"Rogue?" she cried in amazement. "But he's a Texas outlaw. What is he doing so far north?"

"He followed us—it was his gang stampeded the herd."

One consoling thought the captives had, they were traveling west, and therefore must be going in the direction of the herd. Two hours of slow but arduous riding brought them to the outlaws' camp.

Rogue's eyes widened when he saw the last three of the party. "How come?" he asked sharply.

Sullenly the man recounted the circumstances. His coup was not being received with the enthusiasm he had looked for. His chief heard him with an expressionless face until he came to the weapon incident, and then he

Kent Kings: 12 mg. "tar," 1.0 mg. nicotine av. per cigarette by FTC Method.
© Lorillard, U.S.A., 1978
KENT
FAMOUS MICRONITE II FILTER
KING SIZE
Announcing a better tasting Kent.
25% Less tar. Smoother taste, too.
Micronite II filter is why.
Kent. #1 selling low tar. Now even better.
Warning: The Surgeon General Has Determined That Cigarette Smoking Is Dangerous to Your Health.

Newport

©Lorillard, U.S.A., 1977

Alive with pleasure!

17 mg. "tar", 1.2 mg. nicotine av. per cigarette, FTC Report Aug. 1977.

Warning: The Surgeon General Has Determined That Cigarette Smoking Is Dangerous to Your Health.

said:

"So Jim didn't wanta part with his guns, huh?"

The jeer in his voice stung the half-breed. "It would have meant a battle; I reckon I played it right," he retorted angrily.

"You played it safe, anyway," came the sneer. "Awright, I'll talk to Jim now—alone."

"You ain't overlookin' what this means, Rogue?" the other urged. "That's Carol Eden there, an' her dad'll turn over the whole herd to get her back. Why, it's a pat hand. But mebbe this is what you been plannin'? Mebbe Jim and Sandy was fetchin' her in when the Injuns—"

His leader's cold gaze stopped him. "Mebbe you'll mind your own business, Navajo," he said. "When I want your advice I'll surely ask for it. Tell Jim I'm waitin'."

The scowling half-breed slouched to where the girl and her companions were standing and gave the message. When he had gone, the girl turned to her companion and said quietly, "What is going to happen?"

"I dunno," the young man told her. "Jim'll get us out he's a wizard, that fella."

"You seem to think a great deal of him," she said.

"I think more of him than anyone else in the world—but two," he added hastily.

"Your father and mother?" she suggested.

Sandy shook his head. "Dad, yes, but I can scarcely remember my mother."

Jim found the outlaw sitting on a fallen tree at the edge of the camp. He greeted the young man with a hard smile. Jim sat down and rolled a cigarette.

"Howdy, Jim," the outlaw greeted. "Navajo said you wanted to see me."

"Well, I wasn't goin' to let him fancy he fetched me in," Jim explained.

Rogue nodded in comprehension. "Allasame, you've lost out, Jim, and I've won," he stated.

Jim's eyebrows went up. "That so?" he queried. "The game ain't finished yet."

"Talk sense, boy," Rogue retorted. "Sam Eden thinks the world and all o' that girl; I can make my own terms. She's the winnin' card and I hold it."

"But you won't play it," Jim said quietly.

The elder man glowered at him. "The hell I won't! Who'll stop me?"

"You will," came the cool response. "Listen to me, Rogue. Yo're one tough *hombre*—I never met a tougher—but at the bottom you're a man and you can't forget that once you had womenfolk you thought a lot of, an' that there was a time when you'd have shot a man just for speakin' disrespectful of a girl like Miss Eden. She's in your hands by accident; you can't use her to rob her father, *and you know it*."

For a moment he thought the man he had spoken to so boldly was about to spring upon him. The cold eyes had grown hot and the big fists were bunched into knots. But the outlaw held himself in, only his voice betraying the tearing passion which possessed him.

"What's past is past and no damn business of yours," he said thickly. "Why should I care how she comes to be here? To Sam Eden I'm a road agent and cattle thief and if I fell into his han's, even by accident"—with a heavy sneer—"he'd stretch my neck. All right, I ain't blamin' him, but this time it happens to be my turn. I'd be *loco* to pass up such a chance as this, an' what do you suppose my men would say, huh?"

Under his hat brim, the younger man's eyes gleamed slyly. "Hadn't thought of that," he admitted. "Yeah, I reckon you'd find it middlin' hard to persuade 'em."

He saw the other's jaw tighten and his own face remained wooden under the sharp scrutiny it received. Rogue pondered heavily for a while, his brows knitted, and then stood up, motioning the cowboy to follow. The men were gathered in a group listening to the half-breed. They opened out when their leader approached.

"Well, Navajo, you got it figured out to yore satisfaction?" Rogue asked.

The man shrugged his shoulders. "Don't need any figurin'," he replied. "Eden hands over the herd and gits his gal back; that's all there is to it."

The outlaw leader folded his arms, his eyes flinty. "The girl goes back to her father, now, and without conditions," he said deliberately. "I don't war with women."

The decision stunned them to silence for a moment and then babel broke out. Above the protesting voices that of Navajo made itself heard:

"See here, Rogue, we all got a say in this," he cried. "You ain't the only one."

"I've said it," the outlaw told him. "As long as I'm boss of this band I run things my own way."

"*Sangre de Dio!*" one of the gang hissed. "Then it is better we have a new boss, I think."

His arm flashed up, the blue glint of steel along the palm; an instant, and the blade would have been buried in the outlaw chief's breast. But Jim had been watching; a dart of flame from his hip and the knife dropped from shattered fingers. A second later, Rogue's arm fell apart, and with the gun he had drawn from his shoulder-holster, he sent two bullets into the would-be assassin's chest. Staggering, fighting to keep his footing, and mouthing curses, the man went down.

Ignoring the limp figure, Rogue's raging gaze swept the others. He was mad with passion, his whole body—except for the hand that gripped the smoking revolver—trembled with it.

"Who's next?" he barked harshly. "Which of you wants to give me orders? Navajo, you set that coyote on. You got ambitions to fill my shoes. Step out and pull your gun; we'll settle it here an' now."

The other men watched the half-breed curiously. Any one of them might have shot down the challenger but it would have meant a battle, for not all of them were disloyal to Rogue. Also, there was that lean-limbed cowboy, of whose ability to use his gun there was no doubt. Navajo was not the stuff to stand an acid test.

"You got me all wrong, Rogue," he protested. "I ain't makin' trouble, and I reckon the boys don't want none neither. Gittin' the herd is all that matters. It seemed an easy way, but if you got it fixed different, we ain't carin'."

Having gained his end, Rogue was too astute to overplay his hand. He knew the men, understood that self-interest was the only factor which governed their crude natures. Once satisfied that they would not lose, they would be tractable enough.

"I want them cattle as bad as you do—got to have 'em, in fact," he said quickly. "So you needn't worry 'bout that."

Boldly turning his back on them, he walked to the tree trunk. Jim stepped after him. The tempest of emotion which had raged through him seemed to have weakened the outlaw physically; he looked tired and his face was drawn. He was silent awhile, pondering. "How in hell am I to get that gal back to her ol' man? It's most of ten miles. Can't use any of the boys, and I dursn't leave 'em just now."

"Send Sandy, an' you can have my word, and his, that he'll come back—alone." Jim suggested. "You can tell him that my life depends on his doin' that, though there's no need."

"You trust him that much?" the outlaw asked, almost a wistful note in his voice, and when Sudden nodded, "Well, it appears to be the only trail out."

He walked over to where the girl and her companion were waiting, anxiously, for though they had heard the shooting, only Sandy guessed that a man had died. Carol, born of fighting stock, faced the famous desperado fearlessly. With scarcely a glance at her, Rogue said roughly:

"I don't want you here. This fella"— he gestured to Sandy—"will take you back to camp; it ain't so far."

"Thank you," the girl said. "I am sure my father—"

"Don't get any fool notions," he interrupted harshly. "Tell Eden I can win without usin' women." He beckoned Sandy aside. "The herd lies due west—you can't miss it. Now, I want your word that you'll come back—alone. If you don't show up, or bring company; it will go hard with Jim. You *sabe*?"

"I'll be back—if the war-whoops don't get me," the young man promised. "And, Rogue, I wanta say this is a mighty handsome act—"

"Aw, go to hell," the outlaw retorted. "She interferes, and that's all there is to it. Get agoin'."

When they had gone, Rogue came to Sudden.

"What about them guns of yours, Jim?"

"I've pledged myself to stay here till Sandy returns. Don't you reckon it would be wiser to let me wear 'em till then?"

The other considered the proposition; in the event of more trouble with the men, the prisoner would necessarily be on his side.

"Mebbe you're right," he decided.

Meanwhile the girl and her escort were slowly making their way in the direction they believed the S-E camp to lie. Her first words, after they had ridden a mile in silence, took him by surprise:

"Some of those men seemed to know you."

"We'd met 'em," Sandy admitted. "You run up against all sorts when you're driftin' round."

She did not speak again.

In the S-E camp, anxiety at the absence of their young

mistress deepened when neither Sandy nor Jim put in an appearance. A search party was sent out but owing to the redskins' ruse of dividing their forces, was led astray and lost the trail completely on a wide strip of stony ground. Its return without Carol reduced the invalid to a state of blasphemous despair: he cursed everything and everybody, including himself for exposing her to such peril.

Morning broke upon a helpless, and well-nigh hopeless community. The cattleman, propped up by the fire, looked at his foreman in sullen misery.

"Never oughta let her come," he burst out. "Jeff, you gotta find that damn trail. Take all the boys—"

"The herd—" the foreman began, and stopped when the lightning commenced to flicker in his employer's eyes.

"Hey, Jeff, there's a coupla riders a-comin'," Pebbles yelled.

The foreman ran to the speaker's side. Two horsemen were entering the valley at the far end. Jeff studied them for a moment and shook his head in disappointment.

"That ain't Jim's black," he said.

"They might have swapped hosses," Pebbles said hopefully.

"It ain't neither of 'em," Jeff replied, and, as the visitors drew nearer, added, "Why, if it ain't Mister Baudry."

The gambler it was, and with him was a middle-aged, bent-shouldered fellow, with a long horse-face and deep-set sly eyes. With a word of greeting to the cowboys, the pair rode to where Eden was sitting, and dismounted.

Baudry shook hands with Eden and presented his companion: "Meet Davy Dutt; he's in a deal with me."

The cattleman received the stranger without undue enthusiasm—Mister Dutt's exterior was not impressive. Then, in reply to an enquiry for Carol, he told the story of their predicament, and was surprised at the effect it produced; the gambler's full, faintly tanned face took on a yellowish tinge and his voice betrayed real concern.

"My God!" he cried. "Miss Carol in the hands of savages? That's terrible, Sam. What are you doing about it?"

Eden told him and Baudry swore in perplexity. "You can't do a thing till you locate those damned heathens. Got any ideas, Davy?"

"Nope," the stranger confessed. "You seen the kind of country we come through."

The gambler explained that they had been traveling northwest from Fort Worth, and finding a cattle trail some way back, had followed it on the chance of it proving to be the S-E.

The day passed monotonously enough for the little group left in the camp, and when, as the sun sank in the west, the searchers again reported failure to discover the trail of the red raiders, a blanket of gloom descended upon the whole company.

But as the dusk was deepening into dark, Sandy and his charge rode wearily into camp and were instantly surrounded by whooping cowboys. The rancher's eyes bulged when he found the girl he feared was lost forever, kneeling beside him. One arm hugging close, the other hand went to Sandy.

"By heavens, boy, you've put me deeper in your debt than I can say," he cried.

Naturally Carol was the center of attraction; everyone was avid to hear what had happened to her. The story of Jim's slaying of Red Fox brought ejaculations of "Bravo, Jim," and "Good old Texas" from the cowboys, but when she related how they had been rescued from the redskins by some of Rogue's riders, it was Baudry who spoke:

"What's brought that road agent to these parts?" he asked. "Think he's been trailing you, Sam?"

"It would be a safe bet he stampeded our cows," the foreman volunteered.

"But if he's after my herd, why did he let you and Sandy

go?'' Eden asked the girl. ''He must have knowed he had me cinched.''

''I was to tell you that he could win without women,'' she replied.

''Huh! there's two words to that,'' her father said grimly. With the girl safe by his side he was becoming his own dour self again. He looked at Sandy. ''Can you explain it?''

''No, but I'm guessin' Jim fixed somethin', and that's why he stayed and I've got to go back.''

''Like hell you have,'' the cattleman exploded.

''I've promised.''

''A promise to a prowlin' thief don't hold.''

Sandy looked at the girl; in the firelight her cheeks appeared pale; her lips were silent, but her eyes spoke.

''Rogue's word to me was that if I didn't show up it would go hard with Jim,'' Sandy added.

''Did he call him by his name?'' Baudry put in.

''No, he said your friend, '' was the quick reply. ''And because he's that, I'm goin' back—alone.''

The rancher was about to make another angry protest but Carol anticipated him: ''Daddy, he has to go,'' she said, and the young man's heart leapt at the regret in her voice. ''You would do the same yourself.''

The old man snorted, but his hard face softened as he looked at Sandy. ''She's right, boy, of course,'' he admitted. ''You have to do it, but you can tell Rogue that if he harms you or Jim I'll hound him down and hang him, if it takes the rest of my days.''

Sandy grinned. ''I'll pass on the message, but he don't strike me as a man to scare easy.''

An hour later, having fed, Sandy transferred his saddle to a fresh horse and started for the outlaws' camp. He had seen Carol for one moment before he left, had grasped a slim brown hand, had heard a whispered, ''Good luck, Sandy.'' The kindness in her eyes went with him as he rode silently into the gloom.

Eden and the gambler were alone at the fire. The women had retired to their tent and Dutt had expressed a desire to view the sleeping herd. Baudry, biting on a black cigar, was the first to speak.

"Damned if I can fathom Rogue's game, Sam," he said reflectively. "He has you cold and throws the hand in. Why?"

"You can search me," the rancher replied. "Carol figures he has a soft spot, but gals get romantic notions about fellas like him. He's reckoned the most ruthless ruffian in Texas, and that's sayin' a lot."

"Those two men joined you for the drive, dropping in from nowhere," Baudry proceeded. "And one of them—Green—answers pretty well to the printed description of Sudden."

"Whose last job was pulled off while Green was at the S-E."

"True, but it would be a safe play for one of Rogue's men to put the blame on a fellow he knew could prove an alibi."

"You suggestin' that Green and Sandy are in cahoots with Rogue?" Eden asked, and there was a rasp in his voice.

"I'm saying it's possible, that's all," was the reply. "Your daughter said some of the outlaws knew them."

"Then why did them two boys fetch back near a thousand head after the stampede?"

Baudry chuckled. "You have to admit they knew where to find them," he pointed out. "See here, Sam. Mightn't it be that Rogue realized that the stampede was a mistake, that it would pay him better to let you drive the cattle north for him to steal within reach of a market where they'd fetch four or five times as much? Why, that's maybe the reason he ain't forcing your hand now."

The rancher's brows drew together. Put like this the

plan seemed all too probable, and the idea that he was being played with was far from pleasant.

"Tryin' to kill me off don't seem to fit in."

"Why not, if his first scheme was to grab the herd as soon as he could? I'm supposing it was later he got the notion of aiming for the bigger prize, an' I'd wager something it was Green gave it to him; he ain't a fool, that fellow, believe me."

"I don't think you're right, Jethro," Eden said stubbornly.

Baudry smiled. "Well, perhaps not," he said easily. "But I'm telling you, those two men will be back before long; they're more use to Rogue here."

"I'll be glad to see 'em," the cattleman said stoutly, but the seeds of suspicion had been sown. "Aimin' to travel with us, Jethro?"

"Maybe we can be of some use," was the reply.

"Pleased to have you," the rancher said heartily.

The visitor was silent for a time, and then, with the air of one who has come to a decision, he flung the butt of his cigar into the glowing ashes, and looked across at his host.

"Sam, you know what I do for a living," he began. "Well, I'm planning to give myself a fresh deal and drop the cards. With the coin I get when you cash in on your herd I'm starting a ranch—I've got options on land not far from the S-E; with the railways coming west and the northern ranches needing stock, there's going to be money in cattle. But more than that, I want to settle down, with a home of my own—and a wife."

"Why, that's good hearin', Jethro," the rancher said. "Mebbe yo're on the way to fetch the lady, huh?"

The gambler's teeth gleamed as his thick lips parted in a half-smile. "Not exactly," he said. "The lady is traveling north too; in fact, she's less than fifty yards away at this moment."

Eden straightened up, his eyes wide. "You—mean—

Carol?'' he cried incredulously.

''And why not?''

''I never dreamed of it,'' the old man said.

This was true; though Baudry had been a frequent visitor at the S-E, the possibility that the girl was the attraction had not occurred to the owner. Now, faced with the fact, he suddenly realized that he knew very little about the man, save his profession. Still on the right side of forty, suave, well-dressed and apparently wealthy, the gambler did not lack attraction for the other sex, but . . . Sam Eden shook his head, as though in answer to his own query, and Baudry's narrowed, watching eyes grew cold.

''Any objections, Sam?''

''Have you spoken to her?''

''No, I reckoned the square thing was to ask you first.''

Eden breathed his relief; it gave him a way out. Sandy's devotion to the girl was patent, and once or twice he had seen her looking at the boy; women were queer, but he could not conceive that she would prefer the older, sophisticated man for her mate. So he replied with more confidence:

''It's entirely her affair, Jethro. Even if I could claim her as my own child, I wouldn't attempt to influence her. Whatever she says goes, with me.''

''Fair enough,'' he said evenly. ''I'm not asking you to do my courting, Sam. When do you expect to pull out from here?''

''Can't say; must give them boys a chance to come in.''

''They'll do it—with a fine tale of how they hoodwinked Rogue and got away,'' Baudry sneered.

Long after, when he had been lifted back into his bed in the wagon, the words recurred to the rancher. He fought against the fear that they might be the truth, but could not completely convince himself; Baudry's arguments had seemed all too plausible. Moreover, the outlaw's impudent warning that he intended to have the herd was disturbing; Eden was well aware that his outfit was numerically weak and if two members of it could not be depended upon . . . .

nine

Sandy experienced little difficulty in finding the outlaws' camp again. As he rode in, a man with a leveled gun stepped from the shadow of a tree and ordered him to half. A glance satisfied him.

"So you come back?" he said. "Damned if I thought you'd be such a fool."

"It warn't folly, Sligh, just pure affection—for you," was the flippant reply. "What's the next move?"

The outlaw pointed to a small fire apart from the larger one in the center of the glade. Sandy grinned.

"Go ahead," he said. "I might lose my way."

With a curse the sentinel slouched off. Two men were sitting by the fire when Sandy reached it.

Rogue looked up as the boy slid from his saddle. "Hello, Sandy, I'm wantin' that weapon," he said quietly.

Sandy's eyes were on the other figure at the fire. "What's the word, Jim?" he asked.

"You got Miss Eden back?" Sudden queried, and when his friend nodded, he drew his own guns, handing them, butts first, to the outlaw leader. "Ante up, Sandy," he went on. "Rogue has kept his part of the bargain and we gotta keep ours." He smiled sardonically across the flames. "We're your prisoners, Rogue, but I'm givin' you warnin' that we'll light out if we get a chance."

"Then I'll have to tie you," Rogue rapped.

"I don't blame you," Sudden smiled, and at a nod from

him, Sandy relinquished his revolver.

"A bullet apiece would hold 'em better," Sligh snarled.

His chief glared at him. "Fetch these fella's blankets and bring a rope."

The words were quietly spoken but the threat was plain. Sligh knew that in this mood Rogue would destroy him without hesitation. So, without even a sign of dissent, he did as he was bid.

Later, three shapeless, blanket-covered forms lay round the smaller fire. The only difference between them was that two of them were tied hand and foot and appeared to be fast asleep. The third was wide awake, wrestling with the problem of what to do with his prisoners. The disarming and binding had been merely a bluff, for he did not want them; they could only be a burden. The girl had been a different proposition—a weapon—but he could not credit the rancher with great solicitude for two of his hands. Also, Jim had saved his life, and—with all his faults—the outlaw was not ungrateful. Their detention would mean two less to defend the herd, but he dismissed this aspect; his own force was strong enough. A gleam of steel in the flickering firelight caught his eye; it was Sligh's knife, used in the binding and forgotten. It helped him to a decision.

He glanced at the sky, where clouds had now blotted out the moon, flinging a pall of darkness over the camp. Soundlessly he edged over until he was close to Jim, and able to reach the knife. Carefully raising the blanket, Rogue severed the bonds which confined the sleeper's wrists, and dropping the blade, rolled back to his former position. For a time nothing happened and then he saw Sudden stretch and lie still again. Rogue knew that he had discovered that his arms were free.

Presently the dark block of the cowboy's blanket stirred as he slowly sat up. He saw the knife, reached for it, and freed his ankles. With a whispered warning, he did the same for his fellow prisoner. Then, on hands and knees,

Jim crept to the outlaw, whose heavy breathing suggested deep slumber. Leaving their blankets rolled in some semblance of human forms, they crawled away from the fire, and reached the edge of the glade.

"The hosses are on the far side," Jim whispered. "We'll have to pass Sligh. While I deal with him, you slip around an' get the broncs."

Skirting the edge of the encampment, they moved swiftly and silently over the floor of pine needles, and presently saw the sentinel leaning against a pine, his rifle beside him. Like a shadow Jim darted from tree to tree, and then, dropping on his belly, wormed his way forward. All that the unsuspecting watcher knew was that out of the murk a figure rose at his very feet and fingers of steel clutched his throat, imprisoning any sound he might have uttered. A few moments and the man was a limp and senseless weight. Jim let him fall, and hurried after Sandy. That young man had not been idle; he had found the horses and saddles. Soon the outlaw camp was behind them. For a while they rode in silence and then Sandy could restrain his curiosity no longer.

"How in hell did you manage it, Jim?" he asked.

"I didn't," Sudden smiled. "Some kind gent cut my paws loose and left the knife handy."

"Cripes, I'll bet it wasn't Sligh."

"It was Rogue hisself."

"Oh, yeah," came the reply. "Havin' tied us up he would turn us loose, wouldn't he?"

"Them bonds was just eyewash for the gang. Rogue didn't want us—we gotta be watched all the time, and he knows Eden ain't goin' to part with a single steer on our account, so he gets rid of us—his own way. That was Sligh's knife—I saw him drop it; he'll get the blame an' we'll get the credit. Rogue is one smart *hombre*."

A smudge of grey in the eastern sky had turned to a golden glow and the red rim of the sun was pushing above the horizon when they rode down the valley and sighted the S-E wagon. Peg-leg, busy preparing the morning meal, let out a yell which brought men leaping from their blankets and grabbing for guns. When they saw it was not an Indian raid they laughed and swore at the cook. The foreman, his wrinkled face one broad smile, surveyed the pair delightedly.

"Nice damn couple, ain't you?" he said. "Holdin' the drive up thisaway. The Ol Man oughta give you your time."

"And your chin would hit your toes if he did, you holy fraud," Jim retorted. "No, Sandy and me ain't had no sleep for about a year. Who's got spare blankets? We had to leave ours behind."

For a couple of hours they slept like dead men and then Jeff aroused them. "Sam's askin' for you," he said.

They found the cattleman sitting at the end of the wagon. Baudry and Carol were with him, and several of the outfit lingered near.

"Here's the truants, boss," the foreman grinned. "I was tellin' Jim you oughta give 'em their time."

Eden had smothered his doubts and his rugged face softened as he surveyed the men to whom he owed so much. "I reckon they oughta have anythin' they ask for, but I'm hopin' it won't be that," he said. "I'm curious to learn what that ruffian is up to; he had me thrown an' tied. Think we'll hear more of him?"

"Surely. He'll strike when he's ready, but I'm guessin' that won't be till we're nearer a market. He's got nigh a score o' men."

Baudry looked at the cattleman and nodded; he had expressed the same view of the rustler's intentions. With a half-sneer he turned to Jim.

"You seem pretty well acquainted with this cattle thief," he said. "Perhaps he turned you loose too?"

"Now I wonder who told you?" Jim debated. "He did

that very thing."

"Do you mean that, Green?" the rancher asked sharply, and when the other nodded, "Why should he do that?"

The cowboy related the manner of their escape. "You see," he concluded, "we would only have been a nuisance, and besides, I had saved his life a few hours earlier."

"Why?" interjected Baudry.

Jim sensed the hostility in the tone. "If I hadn't Miss Eden wouldn't have been here," he explained quietly. "His men would have had none of his finer feelin's."

"Fine feelings—in an outlaw?" gibed the gambler. "That's more than I can swallow."

"He let her go," the cowboy reminded.

"Yes, at your request," came the sneer. "Were you ever one of his gang?"

"No, were you?" Jim asked.

Pebbles, who was one of the listening riders, chuckled audibly, and the visitor's face flushed with anger.

"Damn your impudence," he shouted. "What do you mean by that?"

Jim bent forward, his eyes bleak. "Just was I said," he replied. "Listen to me, Mister Man. Only two fellas here can talk down to me with safety—my boss and his foreman. You're speakin' outa turn."

For a moment the gambler's narrow eyes clashed with those of the speaker and then turned in mute appeal to his host. Sam Eden was nonplussed. Torn between gratitude and friendship, he did not know how to deal with the tiny tempest which had so swiftly arisen. Carol came to his aid.

"Mister Baudry appears to be forgetting that these two men risked their lives to save me, first from Indians, and then from outlaws," she said. "To my mind, that alone matters."

Like a dash of cold water the words brought Baudry to

his senses; his ill-humor vanished and he achieved some sort of a smile.

"You're right, Miss Eden," he said heartily. "Nothing else counts. I'm sorry, Sam, but I let my ideas run away with me. If that Rogue fellow happened to be here, I'd thank him, whatever his motive may have been."

This ended the discussion, but as Jim and the foreman went to get their horses, the cowboy asked casually:

"You know friend Baudry long?"

"Nope, and you needn't name him my friend neither," Jeff said bluntly. "Don't fancy the fella nohow, an' I'll bet if he had a tail there'd be rattles on it."

"Sandy was right—him and me ain't popular in that quarter," Jim reflected aloud.

"Aw, you should worry," Jeff told him. "So you don't think Rogue will try again yet?"

"I ain't worryin', not that you'd notice," was the reply, and then, "No, barrin' Injuns, flooded rivers, stampedes, storms an' dry stretches, I figure we'll have an easy trip for a while."

Jeff's expression was one of mock disgust. "Yo're a cheerful cuss."

Later, Jim had a word with Sandy. That young man was still puzzling over the outlaw's complicity in their escape, and said so.

"Shake your head and start that stuff you think with workin'," was the smiling advice he received. "Without us, the S-E would be short-handed and Rogue wants the herd to go through yet awhile."

"Then why did he stampede it?"

"I figure his idea then was to sell the cows to the jasper who was payin' him to break the drive. Now, he's aimin' to handle 'em himself and clean up a packet."

"Then he's double crossin' the other man."

"It don't follow. Rogue is a pretty ornery proposition, but he's got points. He told me this fella was willin' to take the S-E cows but he didn't say he'd promised to let him have 'em."

"Glad you put brother Baudry back a bit. What you think of him?"

"I don't," Jim grinned. "But—I'm goin' to."

The cattle, rested by the stay in the valley, made good progress, and the tale of the miles covered grew as the peaceful days passed. The members of the outfit, living in their saddles through the long, lazy hours, became jubilant at the thought that their tremendous task might soon be accomplished.

Sandy was not of the cheeful ones. Baudry's monopoly of Carol was so complete that the young man rarely had an opportunity of riding with her. Moreover, the gambler, as a guest, ate with the women and Eden, a circumstance which did not lessen Sandy's resentment.

Camp was pitched on the tree-fringed bank of a widish river but the fact that it had to be negotiated on the morrow gave them no uneasiness. They had crossed several streams of varying size during the past weeks and had come to regard the operation as of no more than ordinary moment.

"Can you make any sort of guess where we're at?" Jeff asked of Jim.

"Never been north," Jim told him. "This river might be the Wichita, but that don't mean we're clear of the redskins; they hunt all over."

"I ain't worryin' much about the war-whoops—it's that lousy outlaw loses me sleep—not knowin' when he's goin' to strike."

"I'm allowin' it won't be yet," the cowboy assured him.

Two men, seated out of hearing of the camp, were discussing him.

"Those cowboys have to be got rid of, Davy," the

gambler said. "They're liable to make things difficult. Why in hell Rogue let them go I can't guess. What's his game?"

"I'd say he's trying to doublecross us," was the reply.

"If he does, I'll kill him," Baudry said. "No man ever did that to me and got away with it."

There was no anger, no boastfulness in the low, even voice, and well aware that it might be a warning to himself, Dutt, toughened as he was, was conscious of a slight shiver which was not due to the night air. He had no illusions regarding Jethro Baudry, knowing that he would kill his best friend if it suited his purpose.

"I've got the glimmerings of a scheme," the gambler resumed. "Let you know when it's worked out. In the meantime, keep a close eye on those fellows."

At dawn they crossed the river without mishap and resumed the long trek northward. Baudry, as usual, had loped his horse to Carol's side.

"You get more charming every day," he murmured. "This nomad life seems to suit you."

"I love it," she smiled.

"The West is wonderful," he said, "but don't you ever have a hankering to see the real big cities of the world, New York, London, Paris, Rome, with their fine streets, famous picture galleries, palaces, cathedrals, theatres, and to join in the whirl of pleasure they offer?"

"Why, certainly, that would be great, and I expect every girl has such dreams," Carol confessed. "But after a while I would want to come home to Texas."

"Just to go on raising cows," the gambler said.

It brought a faint flush to the girl's lightly tanned cheeks. "Just to go on raising—a new empire," she said quietly. "Yes, Mister Baudry, for that is what the Westerner, rude, ignorant, and frequently criminal as he may be, is doing. Blazing a trail for the millions who will come to replace his sordid settlements with great cities and teach the untamed soil of the wilderness to produce food for the world."

"You're entirely right, Miss Carol, though I'll admit I hadn't looked at it quite that way," he responded. "And I'm proposing to do my share by starting a ranch not very far from the S-E—just to raise cows." He smiled, hesitated a moment, and then, "But first, I'm taking a holiday, to see all the places I mentioned, and others." He leaned across and laid a hand on one of hers. "Will you come with me—Carol?"

Completely taken by surprise, she could only stare at him. He did not wait for a reply.

"I want you for my wife," he said hoarsely. "I'm mad about you—have been since we first met. I'll give you everything you ask for. We'll see all the world can show us and then come back—to Texas. I'm planning big, my dear, but I can swing it; the West is going to hear of Jethro Baudry, believe me."

Carol's eyes opened wide and she shrank from him, dragging her hand from his hot clasp. "But I've no intention of marrying yet, Mister Baudry, and I don't like you—in that way," she stammered at last.

The gambler's face showed his chagrin.

"Perhaps I've spoken too soon. Will you try to care for me, Carol?" he urged. "There isn't anyone else, is there?"

He saw the warm color steal into her cheeks again at that.

"No, of course not," she protested.

"You haven't got notions about any of these scarecrow riders, have you?" he asked keenly, and instantly saw that he had made a slip.

The impertinence angered her. "These men may be poor and ragged, Mister Baudry," she retorted, "but there is not one of them who would do or say anything to hurt me, or who would not risk his life for mine."

"I know it—I'm all wrong," he said contritely. "It's pure jealousy, girl; you've got into my blood. Promise me you'll think it over."

"I would much rather forget it," she replied. "We can be friends."

"No," he cried passionately. It's all or nothing with me. I'm not taking your answer yet. I'll make you care. Do you know what they say of me in the settlements? 'Jethro Baudry always wins—sooner or later.' That's my reputation, and by the Lord, it won't fail me now. I'll not bother you any more now, Carol," he said. "I fancy Dutt is in front; I have a word to say to him."

He rode off, raking his mount ruthlessly with the spurs.

ten

The man was sitting, his back against a tree, his eyes closed. By his side lay a rifle and a saddle, while round his middle was slung a heavy revolver. His thin, harsh face, from which jutted out a beak of a nose, gave him a predatory expression, and a straggling, uncared-for beard lent an appearance of age which his wiry frame belied. It was Jed, riding point, who discovered him.

"Hey, stranger, you have shorely picked a pore place for a nap," he called.

The man opened his eyes. "Hell!" he said weakly. "I was beginnin' to think I was the last fella left in the world. Ain't got a shot of licker, I suppose? I'm about all in."

"Friend," the cowboy grinned, "I've helped hustle these longhorns from near San Antonio. If you think a Texan would carry pain-killer all that way you don't know the breed. I figure you lost your bronc?" The stranger nodded. "The chuckwagon and remuda'll be along presently, they'll fix you up."

In camp that night the stronger told his story. His name, he said, was "Rollitt," and he was horse wrangler to the trail outfit they had followed. One morning he had missed several horses, set out to track them, and had been surprised and chased by Indians. "By bad luck they was between me and the camp," he continued, "so I had to run west. Well, I lost them war-whoops, but I killed my hoss doin' it—just dropped under me—and I lost count o' time too."

Listening to the story, Jim had studied the man closely but could call up no recollection of him. A whispered question to Sandy brought only a shake of the head. Rollitt's explanation seemed likely enough and yet Jim had a feeling that something was wrong. Eden, however, seemed satisfied.

"You've had a tough time, stranger, and I reckon there's small hope of joinin' your own outfit yet awhile," he said. "We lost our wrangler back on the trail; one of the boys has been deputizin' but I guess he'd be pleased to hand over the job. What do you say?"

"Well, I'm surely a maverick and I'm thankin' you," the newcomer replied, and, as the cattleman put a question, "This country is new to me but I figure you should be north of the Wichita. We kept a straighter line, but we got held up and had to hand over cash or cattle. I'd say the longer trip'll pay you in the end."

So it was arranged. Rollitt took over the remuda and appeared to know the work. He did not mix much with the men but was frequently seen in converse with Dutt, who explained that both of them hailed from Missouri. Jim saw little of the man, but as he confided to Sandy, that little was enough.

"What's the poor devil done to you?" Sandy asked.

"Nothin'—yet," was the reply. "You didn't see all Rogue's men, did you?"

"Less than half, I'd say; he had a biggish crowd—scattered, too. You ain't thinkin' this jigger was planted there to wait for us? His story seemed straight enough."

"Too straight, it didn't match his crooked face."

"Hell, Jim, humans ain't permitted to pick their parents," Sandy laughed. "But I gotta admit that if looks count any he'll be the wrong side when they slam the Golden Gates on him."

But Jim was serious. "I've a hunch he's here to make

trouble—mebbe for us."

It was nearly a week later that Jim's forebodings were justified. The foreman, distress signals flying in his face, strode over to where the men were breakfasting and called Jim aside.

"The Ol' Man wants you an' Sandy, pronto," he said. "He's in one of his tearin' tempers; watch your step."

The cattleman was sitting with his back to a wagon wheel. Carol, Baudry, and Dutt were seated near, and standing by was the new hand, Rollitt. Eden's brows bent in a heavy frown when he saw the men he had sent for. He wasted no time.

"Green, how long you been one of Rogue's riders?" he rasped.

"I ain't," the cowboy said coolly.

"Don't lie," the old man roared. "Rollitt here saw you in Rogue's hideout just before you come to the S-E."

Jim looked at the wrangler. "So you *are* one o' his men?"

"Nope, I happened to drift in," the fellow said sullenly. "He made me an offer and I refused it."

"My own case exactly," Jim said drily.

"You were seen workin' with the outlaws, brandin' stolen cattle," Eden went on.

"Those men were feedin' me; I gave a hand," Jim explained. "Besides I was told the cows were mavericks."

"You were mighty friendly with Rogue, an' after you'd gone he gave out that you were on an errand for him."

Jim's eyes sought the informer again. "For a casual stranger you seem to have been pretty deep in Rogue's confidence," he said acidly.

Eden ignored the comment. "An' your 'errand' was to get into my outfit an' help wreck the drive," he said bitterly.

"I appear to have fallen down on that," Jim said.

"Yeah, for your own reasons," Eden sneered. "No wonder you could round up them stampeded steers. Easy, warn't it, when your boss—gettin' a better idea—told you to do it. And then, for some devil's purpose, he lets you fetch my daughter back."

"Make a job of it," Jim urged with savage sarcasm. "Say I was in cahoots with the Comanches too."

"You went after your fellow thief—I'll give you that much credit," the cattleman snapped.

"I'm obliged," the cowboy countered.

Baudry drew a paper from his pocket, unfolded, and held it up. "Isn't this your description?" he asked.

Jim did not need to read it—every word had been branded on his brain as by a hot iron. Nevertheless, he leaned forward and scanned it leisurely.

"Them particulars might apply to a hundred others," he evaded, "And my hoss ain't got a white face."

"Hasn't it?" the gambler rapped out. "I'd like to be sure of that. Rollitt, fetch that black."

Jim's face hardened to stone. "Don't you—unless you want to die," he warned. "Sometime, when he was a colt, I reckon, that hoss had an adventure with a skunk, and he hates 'em."

"Never seen the bronc I couldn't handle," Rollitt growled.

"Go ahead," Jim said. "I'm givin' you permission, but I won't promise to bury you; I don't like skunks neither."

The wrangler hesitated, and was obviously relieved when the cattleman broke in angrily: "To hell with the hoss. Where's the need of that when Rollitt heard you referred to as 'Sudden' by the outlaws? You denyin' it?"

"I'm not denyin' anythin'," Jim said tersely. "And now—what?"

"I oughta tell my men to string the pair of you up to the nearest tree."

The threat stirred Jim to anger. "Come alive, Eden," he

said roughly. "What sort of an outfit would you have left?"

"Showin' your true colors now—gunman stuff, eh?" Baudry said scornfully.

"Lettin' myself be hanged wouldn't prove my innocence," the other retorted. He looked at the rancher. "Eden, you're followin' a false trail," he said quietly. "One of these days you'll find that out. For now—I'm goin'."

The old man did not reply at once; doubts were disturbing him. He could not forget that Sudden had saved Carol from the Indians, but—as Baudry had been at pains to point out—the worst outlaw in the wilds would have done no less in like circumstances. His troubled gaze traveled to Sandy. The youth forestalled him.

"Jim's my friend; if he goes, I do," he said.

The defiant tone roused the rancher's quick temper again. "You're damn right there," he rasped. "But first you'll answer a question. What took you outa camp the night I got this?" He tapped his wounded chest.

Sandy's face flamed at the accusation—for it amounted to that. "You think I creased you?" he cried indignantly, and then, "Hell! what's the good . . . ?"

"I don't think—I know." "Your boss, Rogue, put you up to bump me off, and when you failed, Lasker had to try."

"He'd have got you too, with a second shot, if Jim here hadn't stopped him," Sandy savagely reminded. "You explainin' that?"

"Simple," Eden sneered. "Lasker had bungled it and might have talked. It was a safe play to silence him and get solid with me."

Sandy had no more to say. His world had come crashing about his ears and he could see nothing but the set, pale face of a girl, who, with downcast eyes, had been a witness of his degradation. Baudry, seated next to her, was watching him with an expression of contemptuous amusement. Little did the gambler suspect how near he was to death at that moment. Eden made a violent gesture.

"Punch the breeze, the pair of you," he said hoarsely. "Jeff, you go along and see they don't take nothin' but what belongs to 'em."

At this gratuitous insult, Jim, his thumbs hooked in his belt, shot a scornful look at the speaker. "Don't overplay yore hand, Eden," he warned. "As for your threats, there ain't a man in your outfit would pull a gun on me, 'cept that card-sharp an' his two friends, and they haven't the guts." His cold, appraising gaze traveled from Baudry to Dutt and Rollitt. "Like I said," he added, as they made no move. "Three—yellow—dogs. *Adios!*"

As he turned away, the gambler's hand went to his pistol but the rancher spoke sharply. "None of that, Jethro. Call him back if you want, but you should have took him up when he offered."

The other shrugged his shoulders indifferently, but there was a frozen fury in his voice as he replied, "You're too squeamish, Sam; you don't give a rattler an even break—if you're wise."

In the rope corral which held the night horses Jim and Sandy found their mounts. The foreman watched in silence as they rolled their blankets, and then burst out:

"Jim, I just can't believe it—the Ol' Man must be *loco*. It warn' no use sayin' a word—only have made him wuss."

"I know, ol' timer," Jim said, with a hard smile. "It's a queer yarn—too long to tell now—truth an' lies all snarled up. I ain't blamin' the boss—much; he's sick, an' with Rogue hangin' on his heels, it ain't surprisin' he's suspicious."

"Is it true you're the fella they call 'Sudden,' Jim?

"Yeah, but there's an explanation to that too. Keep a-smilin', Jeff; there was never a rope so badly tangled it couldn't be straightened out.'' From the back of the big black he smiled wryly. ''We'll be seein' you—mebbe,'' he said.

For upward of two miles neither of the outcasts spoke and then Sandy's bitterness overflowed: ''Damnation, even *she* believes I shot the Ol' Man.''

''You ain't no right to say that. You weren't lookin' but I fancy I saw a hand wave from the tent as we left camp.''

Sandy's doleful face changed magically. ''You did, Jim?'' he asked eagerly. His companion grinned too, but for another reason.

''He's just as happy as if she *had* waved,'' he reflected. ''And anyways, he'd do more'n tell a lie for me.''

''Where do we head for, Jim?'' the subject of his thoughts asked. ''We got plenty choice.''

''We have to find Rogue,'' was the unexpected reply.

Sandy stared at him. ''Hell, Jim, you ain't goin' to throw down the Ol' Man, are you?'' There was real concern in his voice. ''I'm admittin' he's treated us pretty mean, but he's been misled, and the boys are our friends.''

''Findin' don't mean joinin',''' Sudden pointed out. ''The S-E is finished with us—or fancies so—but I ain't finished with them. I don't figure on lettin' Rogue beat me, and I'm mighty interested in Mister Baudry.''

''Me too, in fact, I was so interested that I damn near beefed him where he sat.''

''I guessed that and was all set to knock your gun up.''

''Whatever for?'' Sandy enquired.

It would have turned that camp into a slaughter pen. Now, we gotta keep cases on Rogue an' the herd, and be ready to sit in the game.''

Sandy grinned. ''Mebbe you can tell me who pulled the floor from under us.''

''Rollitt is my guess, but who put him up to it?'' Sudden debated. ''Was it Rogue, tryin' to get rid of us, or that tinhorn card cheat? And what's he after, anyways? Hell's flames, it's one fine tangle to unravel and we got only loose ends."

"Here's another," Sandy contributed. "Baudry is goin' in for cattle—startin' a range somewhere near the S-E."

Jim whistled and relapsed into a long silence. At dusk they camped in a dense thicket of scrub and dwarf oak little more than a mile to the right of the herd, with which they have been keeping pace. They were building a small fire when a low voice called, "Howdy, friends!" and a man slid quietly from the shadows. The flickering flame showed that it was Tyson.

"Didn't hear me a-comin', did ye?" he asked, and chuckled at his own cleverness.

"We're glad to see you," Jim said heartily.

"When the business of eating was concluded, the little man filled his pipe and looked quizzically at his hosts. "So the S-E has give you the air?" he remarked.

"They told you?" Sandy queried.

"Ain't talked with 'em," Tyson said. "Here's the how of it. When you busted away and the Injuns took after you, I follered. Bein' on the hoof, I didn't arrive till the fandango was finished. I collects them scalps you left lyin' around, for which I'm thankin' you; worth ten wheels apiece, them top knots is, if you know where to take 'em. Then I trails you, figurin' you're still in dutch and that mebbe I can turn the trick, but I'm too late, you've went. I points for the S-E."

"So you know all about it?"

Tyson shook his head. "I ain't clost enough to hear much but my eyesight is fair and I'm a good guesser," he siad. "When I see Monte Jack in the company I knowed dirty work was afoot."

"Monte Jack?" both his hearers repeated.

"Yeah, fella sittin' next the gal."

"He calls hisself 'Baudry' now."

"Like enough, but he was knowed as Monte Jack in

Kansas City less'n two years ago, and bad medicine. Catched cheatin' at poker and shot the fella under the table—gun on his knees, you know. It warn't the first time an' he had to flit plenty rapid. A close call for Monte, that was."

"An' Eden believes in him," Sandy said.

"Well, you don't have to worry," Tyson laughed. "He fired you, didn't he?"

"Yeah, he fired us, shore enough," the boy agreed. "But there's Miss Carol, that toad's got his poisonous eye on her, and the outfit—decent fellas—are dependin' on puttin' that drive through. They're our friends—still."

"And not likin' Mister Monte Jack nothin' to notice, we're kind o' hankerin' to pile him up," Jim added. He went on to tell of the decision he and Sandy had come to, and the "still-hunter" listened.

"Well, I took a fancy to you boys," he said, when their plans had been made plain. "If yo're willin', me an' Betsy"—he patted the rifle beside him—"will take a hand. Three pairs of peepers is better nor two, and I savvy Injuns."

The cowboys were glad to have him, and said so. Apart from his bloodthirsty occupation, there was a great deal that was attractive in this odd little man. Moreover, they were already deeply in his debt, and neither of them were the type to forget that.

eleven

Early on the following morning Tyson left them. "Hang on to the herd an' I'll be with you come dark, or sooner," he said. Then he plunged into the thicket.

They spent a lazy day, their only concern being to keep under cover; in this the rougher nature of the country helped them, though it increased the risk of running into a prowling band of redskins. Several times, lying flat on a ridge, they got a sight of the herd. And though the distance was too great for him to recognize the rider, Sandy cursed when he saw that Carol had a companion.

The shadows were gathering when Tyson joined them in the dry arroyo where they had decided to spend the night. He had the hump ribs of a buffalo calf, wrapped in part of the skin, and a bow and arrows, for which, he grimly explained, the late owner had no further use.

"I can use her pretty good—lived with Apaches once. She'll fill the pot and save powder."

Tyson had, they learned, located the outlaw band a few miles east, creeping along on the heels of the herd like a mountain cat, ready to pounce on its prey at the propitious moment. He had counted a dozen men, and gathered that others were away hunting.

"They ain't too well fixed for grub and is grumblin'," he said. "A might hard lot. Eden will need all the help he can git, an' then some."

A week passed and save that all parties were nearer their

destination, the position remained unchanged. Then, with the suddenness of a summer storm, danger loomed up, dire and overwhelming.

Tyson had, as usual, after the morning meal, gone to discover possible signs of activity in the outlaws' camp, and his companions were riding leisurely in the wake of the herd. It was Sandy who saw the "still hunter" first.

"Tyson is a-comin' and ain't losin' no time neither," he said.

"Trouble ahead, boys," he panted.

"Rogue goin' to strike?" Jim asked.

"Naw, Injuns," the other replied. "Two score, mebbe even more—they was hidden— waitin' to jump the herd."

"No chance of dodgin' 'em?"

"Not a hope—the cattle has to go that way. Them war-whoops has picked the right place. For miles now the plain is narrow, with rough country both sides. There's one spot where they might hold the herd and make a fight of it."

He described it, and Jim listened carefully. Sandy's face was haggard with anxiety.

"My God! Jim, what can we do?" he asked.

Sudden turned to Tyson. "Climb Sandy's bronc and fetch Rogue," he said. "Don't let on about us; you just happened on the redskins, saw the herd, and figured of course that, as a white man, he'd help his own kind."

"Shore, but I'll get there quicker afoot—it's rough goin'," Tyson replied, and was gone.

Sandy stared at his companion in amazement. "You sendin' for Rogue?" he gasped. The comprehension came to him and he chortled with delight. "You wily devil," he complimented. "That shore is great medicine. Do we warn the S-E?"

"I do; you cross the trail an' follow on the other side, keepin' outa sight. I'll join you later and mebbe the war-whoops'll get a surprise.

Sandy went on his appointed errand while Jim spurred after the herd. The latter passed the remuda in a cloud of dust and heard Rollitt's curse of astonishment. Sam Eden, sitting at the back end of the wagon, greeted the visitor with a glare as he reached for his gun. Jim's cold voice interrupted:

"Don't be a fool, Eden. If I'd come for that you'd be halfway to hell by now. I'm here to tell you that a big bunch of redskins are layin' for you."

The rancher laughed jeeringly. "You don't expect me to believe that yarn, do you?" he asked.

"No, but I had to warn you," Jim retorted. "Walk into the trap if you must; I'll do what I can to get you out, I've sent for aid."

The cattleman's frowning brows went up at this. "Now I know you're lyin'—I'd say there ain't a settlement within a hundred miles. Where'd you send—San Antonio?" he sneered.

"I passed the word to Rogue," was the calm reply.

With the force of a blow, the statement took the rancher's breath away. For a moment he was speechless, and then, with a furious oath, he cried, "So that's your scheme, huh? Rogue's to come and help himself and I'm to let him. Now, listen, I ain't swallerin' your Injuns, but I'd sooner they had the cows than that bastard road agent leader of yours. Get that."

"You seem damned anxious to make your daughter a squaw."

The biting reminder only whipped the rancher's rage to a white hear. "Curse you, I can fight my own battles," he roared. "I don't want your help nor his."

"Allasame, you gotta have 'em. I ain't goin' to see men I have worked with and liked sacrificed to yore bull-headed obstinacy. Can't you savvy that just because Rogue aims to steal your herd later, he's gotta protect it now? Hell, I must put Jeff wise."

The black horse shot ahead of the wagon and with its disappearance the old man's fury evaporated, and the ability to reason returned.

Jim reached the head of the herd and told his news to the astounded foreman.

"A piece along is a steep-walled gully with almost no outlet," he explained. "Throw the cows, wagon, and remuda in there, take cover at the entrance, and wait. When you don't show up, the Injuns'll come a-lookin' for you. If you can stand 'em off for a while, there's help on the way."

"Help?" ejaculated Jeff. "Where in blazes from?"

"I've sent for Rogue," Sudden replied. You see, he's figurin' to lift this herd—presently; so he won't stand by and let the redskins have it."

The foreman's troubled face broke into a grin. "Gosh! that's one bright idea, boy," he exclaimed. "We can deal with that damned outlaw later, but for the time we use him. What did the Ol' Man say?"

"I ain't got time even to tell you what he didn't say," the cowboy smiled. "Get busy, old timer, and if anybody starts shootin' from behind the Injuns you'll know that me and Sandy is sittin' in."

He whirled his horse and raced for the far side of the trail. The foreman's gaze followed him reflectively. "Outlaw, huh?" he muttered. "Pity the damned country ain't got a lot more like him."

Riding ahead, he soon found the spot Jim had described and saw its suitability. The floor of the gully lay below the level of the plain, which sloped into it, and the walls on either side were nearly vertical. The outlet at the far end was too rough and steep even for longhorns to attempt unless badly scared. The entrance was guarded by scrub and rocks which would afford good cover for the defenders. He saw no sign of Indians and surmised, rightly, that knowing the herd must come that way, they were not troubling to watch its progress.

Jeff waited there impatiently, having already given orders for the cows to be hustled along. Soon the leaders appeared, at a lumbering, clumsy trot, bellowing a protest against the unusual exertion. Hurriedly they were hazed into the gully. This took time, and the foreman cast many anxious glances up the trail. When, at length, the wagon and remuda followed the 1st of the cattle, he breathed more freely, and telling the outfit to hunt cover, sought his employer. He found him fuming.

"Ain't I the owner of this herd no more, or are you takin' orders from Green?" was his first question.

"Sure you're the owner, and I'm doin' my best to keep you that," Jeff said tartly. "You gotta remember this, Sam; they may be your cows, but the boys' lives are their own."

"You think that fella was talkin' straight?" Eden demanded.

"Yeah, and so would you if you weren't as prejudiced as hell," was the blunt reply. "Anyways, we'll know soon. The Injuns will have heard the cattle and be wonderin' why we ain't burnin' up."

"Bah! I don't believe—"

The crack of a rifle cut him short and the foreman dashed to the entrance of the gully. The Infant, kneeling behind a ridge, was reloading. He had, he claimed, seen a feathered top knot above a bush some two hundred yards up the trail. Jeff returned to report.

"That scout'll spill the beans," he said, "They'll be along plenty soon."

"Help me outa this and reach my gun," the old man ordered.

With Jeff's assistance he climbed out, walked weakly to the line of defence, and ensconced himself behind a boulder. As Jeff returned for a final glance round the gully,

Carol called him.

"We want to help beat off the Indians," she said.

"I don't, but I'm willin' to," Aunt Judy corrected.

"Can't be did, Miss Carol," the foreman replied. "Yeah, I know you can shoot, but it would worry the Ol' Man into a fit. You can help a lot more by stayin' here an' watchin' the other end of the gully; these devils may steal a march on us thataway and I can't spare a man for the job. Fire a shot if you see anythin' movin' over there an' we'll come *pronto*."

He did not think there was any likelihood of such an attempt, but it kept the girl out of the firing line, and that was all he wanted. As he turned away, Peg-leg came with a message. The enemy had grown tired of waiting. Down the trail from the east came a long line of mounted savages. Each warrior carried the circular shield of buffalo hide, a bow, and a sheaf of arrows. Here and there came the flash of a gun barrel—old-fashioned muzzle loaders, bartered for skins, or gained in a raid on some solitary settlement. Except for an occasional shrill cry, the advance was made in silence.

"Apaches," the foreman decided. "Comanches would have been screamin' their throats out." With the quick eye of one accustomed to count cattle he made a calculation. "Over fifty. Gosh! I'm hopin' Rogue don't dawdle any." He surveyed his slim line of defence anxiously. "Lie close, lads," he warned, "and don't let loose till I give the word; we can't afford to miss."

Baudry, rifle in hand, had joined the cattleman. No one, looking at his passive, unconcerned features, would have guessed that all his carefully planned scheme depended upon the defeat of the redskins. With narrowed eyes he watched the far end of the line swing round until, with one screeching yell, the riders flogged their ponies into a dead run and charged full at the mouth of the gully. Like a wave of destruction the savages surged on and it seemed that the handful of whites must be swept away. Silent, grim-faced with leveled weapons, they waited for the word. It did not come until the foe were less than a hundred paces distant, and then:

"Give 'em hell, boys," the foreman rasped.

The crash of the rifles was followed by exultant shouts from the marksmen as they saw bronze bodies go down before their bullets. The stream of lead disrupted the wave in the center and the two halves curved left and right, replying to the rifles with a cloud of arrows, some of which sang past the ears of the white men. Out on the trail a half-dozen dead or wounded were stretched, and as many horses.

"That'll learn 'em," the Infant cried excitedly, for it was his first real Indian fight. "Do you reckon they've had enough?"

The question was addressed to Jeff, a few yards away; the foreman smiled dourly. "That li'l flurry was only a beginnin', son, sorta appertizer," he replied. "They'll mean it, next time. Keep well down; them arrows can bite."

The redskins were soon on the move again. Strung out in a line they headed west and then whirled and raced their ponies across the gully mouth, each horseman, as he arrived opposite the opening, vanishing from sight.

"Where in hell they got to?" the Infant queried.

"Lyin' alongside the hoss, with a foot through the bellyband," Jeff explained, and added grimly, "Down the hosses, son, an' watch out for arrows."

The caution was needed, for from under the necks of the galloping ponies the red riders sent a succession of the deadly shafts, which whistled through the air and searched the cover. The defenders replied with their rifles, but the moving single marks were difficult to hit, and they did not meet with much success. The braves who had successfully crossed the firing line swung up into their seats again and circled round to repeat the maneuvre. From the far side of the trail two rifles crashed and the same number of ponies became riderless. The foreman chuckled.

"Jim an' Sandy is gettin' *interested,*" he said.

His satisfaction was short-lived. From a clump of thorn bushes ten paces distant came a gasping gurgle and the rattle of a dropped weapon. At the risk of his life, Jeff sprang to the spot, only to find he could do nothing. Crumpled up on the ground, an arrow through his throat, lay Silent. The foreman straightened the body, placed the hat over the face, and swore savagely. As he turned away, the Infant called:

"Hey, Jeff, pull this damn stick out—it hurts like blazes."

An arrow had transfixed the boy's forearm. Snapping the shaft, the foreman drew out the barbed end, inspecting the edges of the wound closely. Then he nodded, and tied it up with a handkerchief.

Mighta been worse," he said. "Keep down; they've got Silent."

The procession of seemingly masterless mustangs had passed and a respite from the rain of arrows ensued. The Apaches were bunched together further down the trail. The intermittent bark of two guns from the rear of the attackers indicated that Jim and Sandy were still interested. At the other end of the firing line Jed was wrinkling his brow.

"Say, Dumpy, haw many d'you figure we've knocked over?" he asked.

"Well, you ain't got any, but the rest of us has downed 'bout ten," was the answer.

For once his friend ignored an insult. "There's more'n twice that number layin' out there an' some of 'em is movin'," Jed asserted.

"Creased and tryin' to crawl clear," Dumpy suggested.

"They wouldn't come this way," Jed objected. "No,

sir, dropped off'n their broncs and playin' dead so's they can sneak in and rush us, that's what. The jigger with the eagle feather in his top knot is five yards nearer than when I spotted him, I'm savin' him the trouble of pertendin'."

Raising his rifle he pulled the trigger and they saw the brown body jerk convulsively, struggle, and flop back.

"Who fired?" Jeff asked sharply. "Wanta kill 'em twice over?"

Before Jed could explain, the supposed corpses did it for him, seven or eight of the nearest scrambling to their feet and sprinting for their lives, zigzagging to escape the bullets the cowboys sent after them. Several were bowled over but the others regained their comrades.

"Good for you, Jed," Eden called out. "I'm remembering it. I reckon they won't try that trick again."

As though they had been awaiting the result of this ruse, the Apaches began to show signs of fresh activity, massing together in readiness for another charge. Two rifles spoke from the opposing side of the trail and a gaudily befeathered brave toppled to the ground, while another jumped clear of his staggering pony.

"Jim an' Sandy," the foreman cried.

"You figure it's them?" the cattleman asked.

"I'm damn sure," Jeff said stoutly. "If we get clear of this it's them you gotta think, like it or not."

The savages were hesitating, the attack from the rear seemed to be bothering them. They were now galloping to and fro, jabbering, gesturing, apparently discussing what action they should take. The matter was to be decided for them. From behind a hillock up the trail a band of more than a dozen riders emerged, spurring their mounts madly, and firing as they came.

At the sight of this reinforcement, the Indians fled. With shouts and wild oaths the newcomers followed, ruthlessly shooting down the runaways. Their leader only did not join in the pursuit. Wheeling his horse, he rode to where the rancher was standing, and got down.

"Well, Eden, I reckon we didn't come any too soon," he said.

"I'd rather you hadn't come at all—we could have beat 'em off without you," the old man ungraciously retorted. "If you're lookin' for thanks you're liable to be disappointed."

"I ain't," Rogue returned drily. "But if you warn't needin' me, why send?"

"I never did. If Sandy came to you—"

"It warn't Sandy," the outlaw interposed. "A little runt of a fella, dressed in deerskin and wearin' moccasins; looked like a forest runner."

"Ain't seen him," the rancher snapped. "I naturally figured Green would use his sidekick."

"So it was his idea, huh?" Rogue said reflectively, and chuckled. "It would be of course. Where is he?"

"I dunno, and I care less," Eden told him. "I set 'em adrift when I learned they belong to you."

"They don't—I wish they did," Rogue admitted. "I could use 'em, but it looks like they're still workin' for the S-E."

"Waitin' for a chance to carry out your orders and drill me again, I suppose?" the cattleman sneered.

"I'd no hand in that, Eden; it's not my way," the outlaw said. His face hardened. "I could take your herd right now if I wanted."

"You could take a slug through the gizzard now if I wanted," the old man growled, gripping his rifle suggestively.

Rogue looked at him in grim amusement. "And what would that buy you? My men, mebbe, ain't got my respect for youth and beauty."

He removed his hat and bowed, either in real or pretended politeness, as Carol—anxious about her father—appeared. Baudry, who had apparently been to fetch her, was just behind. His eyes met those of the bandit leader for one brief instant but his face was devoid of expression.

"We seem fated to meet in unpleasant circumstances, Miss Eden," Rogue said easily, aware that by speaking to her he was rubbing the rancher on a raw place.

"My daughter don't wanta talk to a rustler," Eden said.

The girl gazed reproachfully at her angry parent. "He came to our assistance," she reminded. Her eyes widened as she saw that Rogue's wrist was torn. "You are hurt," she went on, "I've some bandages here—I got them ready, in case . . . . "

"It's only a graze—not worth fussin' over," the outlaw muttered.

But Carol insisted, and Rogue's eyes regarded her curiously as she deftly bound up the wound.

"I'm obliged," he said gruffly.

"I got a scratch too," Navajo put in, his evil, leering gaze on the girl.

Rogue spun round. "Get to hell outa this," he hissed, and before the deadly menace in tone and look the half-breed fell back.

The outlaw leader stepped into his saddle. "Well, so long Eden," he said. "We'll be seein' you. If you bump into any more trouble, send, and we'll come a-runnin'. This time we couldn't help ourselves; next time, mebbe we'll be able to."

With this meaning jest he signed to his men and rode away, indifferent to the threatening growls which greeted it.

twelve

The herd went on, leaving behind one of the oblong heaps of rock which were only too frequently on the Western trails. The rancher was hard to live with during the ensuing days. The loss of one of his men had depressed him; he became moody, savage. The very thought that he had been placed under an obligation to one he despised as an outlaw, who made no secret of his intention to rob him, filled the old frontiersman with fury. He was troubled too with odd doubts in the matter of Green and Sandy. The bandit had disclaimed—more—had regretted them, but probably he was lying. Bah! Green was "Sudden"—a wanted man with a price on his head, and Sandy had tried to kill him, so that was that. Thus he would dismiss the subject, only to find himself milling it over in his mind an hour later.

Baudry also was far from happy, for Carol avoided him. But this was not what most concerned him. It was several days after the Indian attack that he made an opportunity to speak with Dutt alone.

"Well, Monte, you ain't lookin' too peart," was the greeting he received. "What's disturbin' your rosy dreams?"

"I've told you not to use that name," the gambler growled. "So you are satisfied with the situation, eh?"

"Shore I am. Rogue has got this outfit where we want it, an' with those two cowboys in the discard, it looks like pie to me."

"Unless Rogue keeps the cows and sells them himself."

"At that, we're on velvet. Eden's busted an' we get the S-E."

"And that damned outlaw picks up fifty thousand dollars or more. No, Davy, I'm not standing for that. I offered to take those cows at five a head and I'm going to have them. There's another danger, the damn fool is turning soft. Did you see his face when Carol tied his wrist up?"

"He certainly didn't seem to enjoy it as much as—you might—for instance."

"Enjoy it? That was torture for him, it fetched back his past and showed him where he had dropped to. I don't suppose a good woman has stretched out a hand to him for years. She played a big card then, though she didn't know it. I was watching him and I tell you I wouldn't be surprised if he let Eden keep his cows for her sake."

Dutt was plainly incredulous. "Rogue's too tough to fall for a skirt," he said. "And his men wouldn't let him! We can see to it that they don't."

The gambler nodded. "Tell Rollitt to find Navajo and warn him. Rogue must steal the herd. Afterwards—we shall see. My share of that fifty thousand would pay for the wedding trip I have in mind, Davy."

"First catch your bride," the other parodied.

"She'll come to heel, when her father is faced with finding a job," Baudry said. "What do they call it in Texas? Riding the 'chuck line,' eh? She won't let him do that at his age."

Camp was being struck and preparations made for the day's trek when Jim and his two companions made their appearance, greatly to the astonishment of those of the S-E outfit as were present. For days since the encounter with the redskins they had trailed the herd, watched the crossing of a river which Tyson opined must be the Cimarron.

The two cowboys had found the "still-hunter" more

than useful. Not only had he kept them well supplied with game, but his knowledge of woodcraft made him an ideal spy on the outlaws. Unsuspected, moving with the silence of a serpent in the undergrowth, he haunted them, often getting sufficiently near to hear their conversation. But he had not yet learned when they intended to make the final move. Jim, however, guessed that the blow could not now be long delayed, and that was why he had ridden in. The rancher received him with a scowl.

"Eden, I want a word with you," the cowboy said. "I'm goin' to put my cards on the table, an' you'd better look at 'em."

Very briefly he told the tale of his adventures to the time he joined the S-E outfit and the smile on the gambler's lips became more pronounced. When Jim paused, he laughed outright.

"Damned good," he jeered. "You ought to be writing dime novels. Why didn't you come out with this fine story then?"

"I couldn't prove it," Jim said simply. "And I wanted to get outa the country."

"I'll bet you did," came the jibe. "Besides you were working for Rogue."

Jim raised his shoulders. "This fella claims he's goin' to ranch near you," he said to Eden. "Did he mention his brand?" The old man shook his head. "Well, it don't signify—he told your daughter. See here."

He picked up a half-burnt stick from the fire and in the sand at his feet traced the letters, S-E. Then he joined up the ends of both, turning them into 8-B.

"That's his iron," he said quietly. "Convenient, ain't it?"

Baudry's expression of amused indifference vanished. "By heaven, Sam, I never thought of that," he cried. "Comes of not being a cattleman."

It was well done, but his laugh met with no response;

brand-blotting was not a subject of mirth in that company.

"Yeah," Jim said ironically. "While I was staying with Rogue, his men brought in a bunch of cattle to brand. As I told you, they were feedin' me, so I did my share. They were supposed to be mavericks, but most of 'em was S-E when they was thrown and 8-B when they got up."

"Which only proves that Rogue was taking advantage of my ignorance to sell me stolen steers," Baudry pointed out. "Till the other day I'd never seen the fellow. I let it be known I wanted stock and took it for granted they would be unmarked strays."

"Rogue told me a man was payin' him to bust this drive and was willin' to take all or any o' the herd," the cowboy went on. "Who gets your ranch, Eden, if you fail to put your cattle through?"

Baudry reached out a cigar, lit it, and laughed.

"Dime novel stuff," he said. "Prove it."

"Right," the other rejoined. "Eden, I want your hoss-wrangler, Rollitt."

The foreman returned with the wrangler, whose shifty eyes widened when he saw the visitors. "You wantin' me?" he asked his employer.

"How long you been in with Rogue?"

"Ain't never," he growled. "What you gettin' at?"

"The truth," Jim retorted. A gun seemed to leap into his hand. "Rollitt, I'm givin' you a chance to come clean. If you don't, I'll kill you." The cold, merciless tone drove the threat home. The wrangler's gaze traveled round the circle of faces. "Nobody can help you," the icy voice went on. "Whatever happens to me, you'll be as dead as Moses."

Rollitt looked at the leveled gun. "Mebbe it's a year," he said huskily. "I broke away—"

The gun roared and a line of red on the man's cheekbone showed where the bullet had grazed him.

"The next lie will be your last," the marksman warned.

"You've been watched, you fool. What was the word you took from that man"—he pointed to Dutt—"to Navajo?"

The nearness of death had shattered the ruffian's nerves. With trembling lips he mumbled the message: "Rogue is sellin' you; get busy with the boys and strike quickly."

"That's a—" Dutt began, and promptly subsided when he saw Jim's eyes upon him.

"Well, Sam, are you taking the word of this gunman with a price on his head against me, Jethro Baudry, a respected citizen, and your friend?" the gambler asked coolly.

Before the rancher could reply, another voice chimed in, and the little Indian hunter thrust himself forward.

"Jethro Baudry, huh?" he piped. "When I see you in Kansas City not so far back you was Monte Jack, a card cheat who skipped outa town two-three jumps ahead of the Vigilantes, wanted for killin' a sucker you'd trimmed—shot him under the table, didn't you?"

Except that it was a shade more pallid, the gambler's face did not alter. "You are mistaken, my friend," he said.

"Monte had a scar runnin' up his right arm from wrist to elbow, where a Mexican had tried to slip a knife into him. All red and puckered it was, like the edges had been sewed up clumsy."

"Roll up yore right sleeve."

It was Jim who gave the order, and his gun was again out. Baudry's face was livid; he knew the game was up—for the moment.

"No need—the scar's there," he admitted, and turned to Eden. "You win—for now, but don't forget I hold your paper."

The rancher, whose rage had been steadily rising at the revelation of how he had been duped, boiled over at this.

"You dirty thief," he cried, and gripped his gun.

The threatened man jeered. "It would be a good way of

paying your debt, wouldn't it?"

Eden's fingers released the weapon as though it had been red hot. He glared at the scoundrel who had gauged him so correctly. "You'll get your money—every cent of it—when I sell the herd," he promised.

Baudry's lips curled in a wolfish snarl. "I don't propose to," he replied. "I'll have the money, the S-E, and—anything else I want of yours." His eyes went to Carol as he made the insolent boast. "You damned old fool," he gritted, "I'll make you curse the hour you quarreled with me. I'll break you and grind your face in the dust. When Rogue has done with you—"

"Rogue can speak for himself, Mister," came a quiet voice.

The outlaw was standing there. So absorbed had everyone been in what was taking place that they had not seen him ride in and dismount.

"Far as I'm concerned, Eden, yore herd is safe," he began. "I can't speak for my men; that toad there has poisoned 'em and they've named a new leader."

"So you sneak off here to save your hide?" Baudry sneered.

The outlaw's eyes flashed. "Best take care of your own," he said. "I don't owe you money." He looked at Eden. "Jim has given you the straight of it," he went on. "What you aimin' to do with these rats?"

The cattleman gestured angrily to his foreman. "Clear 'em out," he ordered, and to Sudden, "Green, I'm takin' your word, but you ain't told who drilled me."

Sudden looked at Rogue, who shook his head. "I don't know," he replied. "But it wasn't Sandy."

The rancher turned his hard eyes on that young man. "I ain't convinced," he said stubbornly, "but I'm willin' to be."

A word from the foreman sent the other men about their tasks, leaving the boss and the outlaw alone. An awkward silence ensued, broken at length by the visitor:

"Studying why I'm here, Eden?" he asked. "If you think it's because of that scum over there you got another guess comin'. I'd have shot it out with 'em, but I thought I could undo some of the harm I done you."

The rancher's expression was frankly skeptical.

"Don't believe me?" the outlaw went on. "Dunno as I blame you, but it's a fact. Ain't you wondered why I let you get so far after that fandango with the Apaches? Well, I've been tryin' to persuade the boys that it would be a better play to let you sell the cows and then lift the dollars, trustin' you could find a safe place for 'em. That card sharp put a crimp in that and here I am. What you gotta say?"

"You can stay, but my men'll have orders to shoot you at the first sign of funny business," he decided.

"That's only fair," Rogue said, and walked away.

thirteen

The country stretched before them, flat, brown, uninteresting, but the trail drivers found it satisfactory, since no danger could approach unseen. The herd, spread out fanwise, moved slowly forward and Sam Eden—able to sit in a saddle again—pulling up his pony to watch the beasts pass, exulted as he noted their fine condition. Then he frowned as he remembered that catastrophe might yet overtake them. Behind the drag, Rogue was riding alone. The rancher joined him.

"What d'you figure them coyotes will do?" he asked bluntly.

"We talked it over," the outlaw replied. "To attack on the march would surely mean stampeding the steers; we'd have to gather 'em again and might lose quite a number—not all my men knows cattle. The other way was to wait till the herd was bedded down and rush your camp after dark; the night riders could be easy dealt with later. I'd say that's what they'll try, and it'll be soon, mebbe tonight."

The rancher was silent for a while, furtively studying the hard face of this desperado who had striven for his ruin and was now, apparently, eager to help him. He could not understand it, and still suspected double-dealing.

"What you know of that fellow Sandy?" he asked.

"Mighty little," was the reply. "He drifted in one day, a piece before I met up with Green, and hung around. Didn't mix well with the rest—too clean, I reckon." He smiled and shook his head. "No harm to him: just a boy gone a bit wild."

Evening brought them good fortune in the shape of a disrupted strip of plain, with a camp site which could be defended.

Supper was eaten almost in silence, and hurriedly, each man with his rifle beside him; at any moment he might have to jump up and fight for his life. Then the women were sent to lie down in the wagon and Eden posted his men, with a grim word of warning:

"Don't shoot till you're sure," he said. "Then—get 'em." It was nervous work kneeling there behind the barricade, waiting. Sandy, squatting beside his friend, voiced his thoughts.

"I hope they show up—we won't find such a good place in a hundred miles."

"I'm bettin' they do—it's pretty near their last chance, and with no moon, they'll figure on a surprise."

"They'll get it too," Sandy chuckled. "Where's Tyson?"

"Saw him siftin' into the brush," Jim replied. "Gone to smell 'em out for us; he's a four-eyed wonder in the woods."

The cowboy's guess was a good one. As soon as he had eaten, the forest runner, with a word to Eden, had faded into the shadows, leaving his beloved Betsy behind. Now, prostrate on his belly, he wriggled a way through the brush, ears attentive to the slightest sound. For an hour or more he heard nothing.

Then came a noise, one he had been expecting—the crack of a snapped dry twig, directly in front. Rising to his knees he drew the long, keen blade from his belt and waited. The bush beside him shook and a man on all fours appeared, pushing his rifle ahead of him. Swiftly, silently as a striking snake, the knife flashed and the victim, without even a groan, flattened out like a prickled bladder.

Rollitt would rob no more.

A muffled curse away to his left and another cracking of dried wood on his right told him that the marauders were getting close; he must warn the camp. With infinite caution he retraced his path; no one of the watching outfit saw him return, but the word was passed along.

Tense moments ticked by and from behind a cactus a shadowy, indistinct form appeared gradually to grow out of the ground. It saw what it expected—the glow of a fire, and round it, dark shapes of sleeping men. A low whistle brought other shadows, and then a dozen guns shattered the silence of the night, driving bullets into the artfully arranged blankets. To the attackers' surprise, no reply came.

"We must have got most of 'em—there'd be several with th' herd," Navajo reasoned. "Come on, fellas."

Confident of success, the outlaws emerged from concealment and dashed forward. This was the moment for which Eden had been waiting.

"Now," he called sharply.

From behind the barricade, guns spat in a spiteful chorus and in the advancing line men dropped silently, or stumbled and cursed as they fell. Their leader, realizing that they had walked into a trap, turned and raced for cover again, calling to his men to do the same. A number succeeded, but motionless black blotches on the ground told that the attacking force had suffered. Silence again ensued, broken only by an occasional shot when a cowboy fancied he detected a movement in the scrub. Navajo was cursing.

"They was waitin' for us, burn their souls," he grated. "Somebody musta tipped 'em off—them fallin' trees wasn't no accident. I'm bettin' it was Rogue, the . . . Hell! th' moon'll be up in less'n half an hour and they'll be able to pick us off like cotton tails. We gotta rush 'em before then—it's our only chanct."

The charge was made, and met—as before—with a leaden shower, but this time the attackers were desperate. Though several dropped, the rest came on, climbed the barricade, and leaped down upon its defenders.

Jim, having fired his last shot bringing a man down, slipped aside just in time to get his head out of the path of a swinging rifle butt. Before the wielder of the weapon could recover his balance, the cowboy stepped in and drove a venomous fist to his jaw. The fellow collapsed limply, dropping like a sack of meal, and at the same instant, clawlike talons encircled Jim's neck from behind, sinking into the flesh and shutting off his breath.

"Got you, you damned spy," came a hiss.

It was Navajo. With all his weight on the cowboy's back he was striving to fling him to the ground. With groping fingers he tried to loosen the half-breed's hold but it was of no use. Then, in despair, he savagely jabbed an elbow backward into the body behind him. The result was magical; caught fairly in the solar plexus, Navajo's hands fell away, and he tottered back gasping, helpless.

For some seconds the cowboy could do no more than suck air into his starved lungs, and then, seeing that his enemy was recovering, he ripped across a blow which sent the outlaw reeling to earth. Snarling curses, he sprang up, and as Jim ran in, flung a handful of sand in his face, and bolted. For the moon was up and a quick glance had shown him that his men were scuttling like rabbits. Completely blinded by the stinging particles of grit, Jim could do no more than express himself, stamping about, dabbing his smarting eyes with his neckerchief.

The foreman arrived, bringing the news that save for sundry slight wounds and bruises, the outfit had come out of the ordeal unscathed. "I reckon we've discouraged them cattle thieves a whole lot," he concluded grimly.

He was a long, scraggy fellow of middle-age, with a thin humorous face, and his rigout proclaimed that he had recently visited a settlement, clothes, saddle, and weapons being patently new. He came into view as they were about to bed down the herd, and Eden rode to meet him.

Karson—so the stranger named himself—told the rancher that Abilene was less than a dozen miles distant. He himself had ridden out to the herd, having been advised that it was on the way.

"I'm in these parts to buy cattle," he said.

"I'm here to sell 'em," Eden replied, not too eagerly. To have reached the goal first strengthened his position and he meant to take advantage of his luck. Moreover, the experience of the past few months had made him distrustful.

The cattle buyer slept in camp, having decided to accompany them on the final day's march. He advised that the herd be halted a couple of miles short of Abilene, where there was good grazing.

Darkness was still distant when they sighted a haze of smoke on the horizon and realized that the end of the long trail was within reach. When the cattle were bunched and bedded a small party was headed for Abilene; Karson, Eden, the women and Sudden.

They reached the town as dusk was falling. Karson conducted them to his hotel, where they secured rooms and dined. Then he carried the cattlemen off to "take in the town." Eden, having warned his daughter to remain indoors, told Jim he was at liberty to amuse himself. The cowboy did not like this arrangement, but could hardly protest.

Leaving the hotel, he mingled with the motley mob streaming along the street. At the door of the Palace Saloon he hesitated a moment and then went in. A blear-eyed individual sidled up to him.

"You're a stranger," he accused, shooting out a grimy finger.

"You must be a magician," the cowboy quizzed.

"I ain't, but I savvy all the fellas in this here burg," the other replied.

"I'm the town marshal of this here city," he began pompously.

Jim regarded him gravely. "That so? What am I supposed to do—throw a fit—or somethin'?" he enquired.

The marshal's bloated face got redder. "I can tell you what you ain't s'posed to do and that's wear them guns," he snapped. "It's agin' the law. I'll trouble you to hand 'em to me."

Sudden's eyes narrowed. "I hate trouble," he said. His gaze swept over the room, noting that nearly every man in it wore a weapon. "Why start on me? Clean up on them others and—I'll think about it."

"You're a newcomer; I know them fellas," was the lame reply.

"Yeah, that's where the rope rubs—I don't know 'em," the cowboy said quietly. "See here, Marshal, I'm attached to my guns an' they're attached to me,"—he smiled—"partin' would be—difficult."

The keeper of the peace went in search of another, and presently Sudden saw him in converse with two men whose entrance he had not noticed—Baudry and Dutt. Even as he caught sight of them they were moving toward him. The gambler opened the ball:

"Yes, Marshal, that's the man," he said. "Known as 'Sudden' in Texas, and wanted for cold-blooded murder and robbery."

"And that fella, Marshal," parodied the cowboy, "is Monte Jack, a tinhorn who was run outa Kansas City for shootin' a pilgrim he had cheated."

Baudry drew himself up. "That's not true," he protested.

"This is," Jim rasped, his open hand striking the gambler on the cheek with a crack like a pistol shot. Staggering back under the force of the blow, his face livid with passion, Baudry clawed at his shoulder-holster. Dutt flung his arms round him.

"Don't be a fool, Monte, he'll get you," he cried.

At the name unwittingly used the marshal's piglike eyes widened. He snatched out his own gun.

"If there's any shootin' here, gents, I'm doing' it," he announced. "Settle your differences outside."

"Good enough," Jim said, and looked at Baudry. "At eight tomorrow mornin' I'm walkin' down the street; if you ain't lost yore nerve and skipped by then, you can come and meet me."

"I'll be there," Baudry spat out.

Followed by curious glances—for the fracas had attracted attention—Jim left the saloon. At the hotel he found Eden and told him only that the gambler was in town.

"Glad of it," the rancher siad. "I can square my account with the dirty sneak an' be a free man again."

Abilene, on the following morning, presented an unwonted appearance of emptiness, save on the sidewalks of the principal street where a number of daring souls had lined up. For the news of the challenge had quickly spread and a crowd had come to see one man kill another, and to wager on the result.

An excited whisper ran through the throng when, on the stroke of eight, the cowboy walked from the hotel to the middle of the street. That he was a famous gunman from the South was already known to all. For an instant he stood there, his arms hanging down, fingers almost touching the butts of his guns. Silence seized the spectators as, a hundred yards away, another man was seen to be unhurriedly approaching. So the gambler had not gone. Jim's lips tightened.

The seconds ticked on, each bringing one of the men, or both, nearer eternity. The onlookers gazed breathlessly as the gap between the combatants lessened. Then the angry bark of a pistol smashed into the silence and Jim's hat was swept from his head. Almost without looking, the cowboy drew and fired, and a man who had stepped into view round the corner of a store reeled and went down, his smoking gun clattering on the boards. It was Davy Dutt, and a howl of disgust came from the nearest spectators when they realized the treachery he had attempted. Jim himself, bareheaded and swinging the revolver loosely in his fingers, paced steadily on. He had eyes only for the man he was going to meet.

To Jethro Baudry, the failure of the plot was a crushing blow; it had seemed so sure and easy to explain; an unknown enemy, seizing the opportunity to pay a debt. Why had Dutt let himself be seen, and above all, why had he missed? Savagely he cursed the man who had died for him.

Step by step the cowboy came on, relentless, inevitable as death itself. Forty yards—thirty—twenty—damnation, would the fellow never stop? He felt like a condemned criminal, awaiting execution, and watching the leaden hours creep by, but in his case they were moments, seconds, and at that thought he pulled up.

"Can't miss at this distance," he muttered.

He tried to raise the gun he was carrying but found he could not; it seemed to weigh a ton. His antagonist was now only a dozen paces away. Desperately he made an effort to fire but his paralyzed muscles refused to act, and in a panic of frenzied fear, he dropped the weapon, flung up his arms, and bolted. Staggering, slipping in the loose dust, expecting every instant the numbing jar of a bullet in his back, he did not hear the yell of derision which followed him as he vanished behind a convenient building.

The cowboy watched him go, a mingled expression of contempt and doubt on his face.

"I figured him right," he said to himself. "Allasame, I'd oughta got him." On returning to the hotel, he found Eden and the buyer ready to ride out and inspect the herd.

"I'm glad you didn't kill him, Jim," the rancher said. "It would have looked like you were payin' my debt."

"It may come to that yet," Jim told him.

"You don't think he's finished?" Eden asked.

"There's only one way to keep a rattler from bitin'," was the meaning reply.

When they reached the camp, Eden had the cattle lined out and driven past, he and the buyer counting independently. Their figure nearly tallied.

"Call it two thousand, two hundred," the rancher offered.

"Good enough," Karson nodded. They're a likely lot and in fair fettle, but I only want four-year-olds—twenty-five a head.

Eden's face fell; this meant taking the pick of his herd and leaving him with the less saleable residue.

"That ain't a square offer an' you know it, Karson," he said bluntly. "Gimme an all over price of twenty and take the lot. With the northern ranches yelpin' for stock, you can't lose."

"It's a deal," Karson replied, aware that he had made a good bargain. "Of course, your boys'll hold the herd here till I can arrange for shippin'? Good."

The news that the steers were actually sold caused great jubilation among the cowboys.

They saw nothing of Rogue. He had, the foreman said, ridden off the previous afternoon and had not reappeared. The news brought a frown to the rancher's face; he still distrusted the outlaw.

When the party returned to town, Sandy—at Sudden's suggestion—went with them. Eden was to receive payment for his cattle at once, and had announced his intention of taking charge of the money himself. Banks were few and far between in Texas and he had little faith in such institutions. So he tucked the big roll of bills into an inside pocket and tapped the butt of his gun meaningfully.

"Any fella who tries to lift those off'n me will surely get a shock," he boasted.

In the back room of a Mexican dive at the other end of the town, Navajo, with contemptuous amusement on his thin lips, listened to the stumbling excuses of the man before him.

"Can't think what came over me, but I couldn't have raised my gun for a million dollars," Baudry said. "Never felt like it before; I must have been sick."

"You sure looked it, but for a sick man, you ran almighty well," the half-breed sneered.

The gambler's eyes grew malevolent. "I'm not sick now, Navajo," he warned.

"Glad to know it," was the reply. "You'll be better able to bear the shock of hearin' that Eden has sold his herd and got the money. To put it plain, we're beat."

"Quite a slice of that money is mine," he said, "and do you know, I believe the old fool will pay up."

"Better ask him, but mind Mister Sudden ain't around or you'll be meetin' Dutt mighty soon."

"So it was Davy?" the gambler mused. "I suspected it. Well, he was always fond of me. How many would do a thing like that for you, Navajo?"

"Not one, even if I asked," the half-breed replied. "I do my own dirty work."

"But you got Lasker to shoot his boss," came the reminder.

"I offered him a price—same as you did me," Navajo said sullenly.

Baudry's brows went up. "You are in error, my friend," he pointed out. "I made a bet with you—quite a different thing, and you look like you're losing it. I shall deduct the amount from your share of the herd money."

The outlaw straightened up. "You are goin' to get it?"

"What else did you think?" the gambler retorted. "Yes,

I am going to get it—the money, the ranch, the girl, trample Eden in the dirt, and kill that damned gunman."

"Oh, yeah," the half-breed gibed. "You'll do some swingin' if you show your face in town; that frame-up ain't made you one bit popular. Well, let's hear your plan."

For some time Baudry talked earnestly, and when he had finished, sat back and looked triumphantly at his confederate.

Navajo nodded. "You can count me in," he said shortly.

His malignant gaze followed the gambler as he went out. "Yellow-bellied coyote," he muttered. "You'd sell your own sister for ten cents, and right now yore figurin' to doublecross me. That's a game more'n one can play at, and when I pull a gun, runnin' won't save you."

fourteen

Soon after dark that same evening, a Mexican lad slid into the Palace Saloon and made his way to where Eden and Sandy were watching a game of poker in which Karson was taking part. Twitching the rancher's sleeve, the boy whispered:

"Meestair Green wantin' you, *pronto*—outside."

Eden started for the door, and Sandy stepped after.

"No need to drag you away, boy," the cattleman said.

"I'm comin'," Sandy replied. "Jim's word was to stick to you like your shadow."

"Shucks, I've had too much nursin' lately," Eden laughed, and as he stepped into the street and looked round.

A blurred shape detached itself from the gloom, an arm snapped viciously down and the rancher dropped like a pole-axed steer. Sandy grabbed at his gun but before he could get it out, three men sprang upon him. Uttering a yell for help, he flung his fists right and left. His shout brought other citizens and these hurled themselves enthusiastically into the battle. Since they knew neither the cause nor the combatants, they were soon fighting each other, and were of no use to those they had come to assist.

Standing astride his employer's body, Sandy struggled on, wrenching himself free from clutching hands and driving his fist vengefully into indistinct faces. But it could not last. Almost spent with incessant effort, he was rapidly weakening. From behind came a bitter oath in a voice he remembered, but before he could turn, a sweeping blow with the barrel of a pistol sent him down.

It was at this moment that Jim heard that there was trouble at the Palace, and came to investigate. He found an excited group outside, many bearing marks of the conflict, gathered about two senseless men.

"What happened?" he asked a bystander.

"Durned if I know," was the reply. "There was a shindy, so I sat in—never could keep outn' a scrap, nohow. Then three-four fellas ran away an' I found I was fightin' a fightin' a friend. Do you know them *hombres*?"

The light of a match confirmed the cowboy's fears. "Hell, yes, one of 'em is my boss," he said, and made a hurried examination. "They ain't cashed, anyways."

Karson was found, and the injured men carried to the hotel.

"This is a bad business, Green," the cattle buyer said. "I suppose they got the money?"

"Reckon so—it's gone."

"He was askin' for it; you can't keep anythin' quiet in this place. It was known he'd sold his herd and these scallywags took the chance he'd have a fat wallet. I oughta stayed with him but poker's a fair curse with me."

Jim did not undeceive him. His own mind was full of conflicting conjectures. Baudry, Navajo, or even Rogue might have planned this latest development, and that it was one or more of them he was convinced. Bitterly he reproached himself for allowing the gambler to escape.

Jim returned to the sick room. Eden was still unconscious, but breathing easily. Sandy was in a fever to see his friend.

"Jim," he cried, "Navajo was there—I heard his voice. Damnation, they've got Carol. What we goin' to do?"

"You'll stay here," Jim replied. "I've got a line on the

girl and I'm goin' after, right now."

He told him that Aunt Judy said a woman called Lily Gold called for Carol and they left together.

He found the house, a two-storied, ramshackle frame building. The door was opened by a stout, middle-aged black woman.

"Mis' Gold is upstairs but she ain't seein' nobuddy," she told them.

"She'll see us," Jim said, and slipping a coin to the woman's hand, pushed past.

They found Miss Gold smoking a cigarette and lolling in an armchair. Not yet thirty, she still had charm of a kind, but her once pretty face had become hard, predatory, and her yellow hair was obviously dyed. She greeted her unannounced guests with a stare of surprise.

"And who the hell may you be?" she asked belligerently.

"That don't matter," the cowboy said. "We want to know what you've done with Miss Eden?"

"Don't know the lady," the girl replied insolently, but there was a flicker of fear in her eyes.

"Lyin' won't help you," Jim said evenly. "We know that you called on her an' that she left the hotel with you."

"Oh, that kid," she said. "I showed her round a bit and then she said she wanted to do some shopping. I expect she had a fella to meet."

The girl was shaking when she saw Sudden's grim expression.

Then the story came tumbling out. She had been paid to lure the victim to a certain Mexican dive, the bait being that a cowboy named Sandy had been badly hurt in a brawl. Two men had met them there, seized Miss Eden and ridden away. One of the men was Baudry; the other a stranger.

"Where have they taken her?" Jim barked.

"How the hell do I know?" the woman snapped, and

then shrieked as a knife gleamed before her eyes.

"There's an old shack out on the plain, about two miles due north," she gasped. "I heard them mention it. That's all I know. Get out, damn you! Get out!"

In a lonely, tumble-down cabin to the north, lit by a guttering candle, two people were facing one another. Carol Eden, her hands bound, leaned against the wall, contemptuous, defiant.

Baudry, seated upon a box, regarded her with a smile. He had sworn to have her and here she was. Soon they would be away—headed for civilization, and by the time they reached it. . . . Affairs had not gone quite as he had planned, but with the girl, the herd money, and the mortgage on the S-E in his possession, he would take most of the tricks. But first he must deal with the half-breed, the man who had jeered at and taunted him.

"Sit down," he ordered, pointing to a second box on the other side of the table.

"I prefer to stand," Carol replied. "I can keep farther away from you."

The man smiled tolerantly. "When you're my wife, you'll know me better," he said.

"Impossible!" she cried. "What else are you besides, liar, cheat, and coward?"

This time the scorn in her low vibrant voice seared him. He stood up and stepped towards her, slowly, like some wild beast about to pounce on its helpless prey. Staring at him with fear-wide eyes, she backed away until she could retreat no more. The gambler's gaze dwelt gloatingly on the lissome, rounded form.

"I'm a man who can tame women and make them do as I wish," he said softly. "In a little while you'll come creeping to me for a kind word and be happy if you get it, though now you dislike me."

The nearness of her intoxicated him and he laughed as his hands darted out, prisoning her arms. The feel of the firm flesh beneath his fingers fired his blood and sent his hot lips questing for hers. Mad with terror and loathing, she fought to avoid them, but bound, and held in that grip of steel, could do little. The brute's liquor-laden breath sickened her. He tore open her shirtwaist and rained kisses on her bared neck.

"I'll teach you," he panted thickly.

And then, when she had given up hope, he flung her violently from him. A horse had whinnied outside.

Dazed and weak, Carol saw her assailant fall into a a half-crouch, his gun drawn, death in his eyes. She tried to shout a warning but no sound issued from her dry, throbbing throat. The door was flung open, Baudry fired, and the newcomer stumbled, coughed, and slithered to the floor, a pistol dropping from nerveless fingers. After a moment's pause, the killer bent over him.

"Rogue?" he muttered. "Wonder how he got wise? Well, that's a debt I was afraid I'd have to leave unpaid. Where the hell is Navajo?"

"Right here," the half-breed replied from the doorway, and stepped noiselessly into the cabin. His mean eyes rested callously on the supine form of his late leader. "That saves me a job but I ain't thankin' you."

"Did you get Eden?"

"I reckon—'less his head's made of rock," the ruffian replied. "The crack I gave him would have split the skull of an ox."

"Hope you haven't overdone it," Baudry said viciously. "It will hurt him more to live."

"Mebbe, but that fella Sandy came out of the saloon with him and fought like a wildcat. We corralled the cash."

Dull despair took possession of the prisoner. Her father injured, probably dying, and Sandy . . .

"You did well, Navajo," the gambler said. "If we'd got the devil, Sudden, it would be a clean-up."

"I'll tend to him," the other said darkly. He threw a roll

of bills on the table. "We split that two ways and then settle about the gal."

Baudry jerked round as though he had been spurred. "She goes with me," he answered harshly.

"Mebbe, after we've cut the cards for her," Navajo replied.

"Have it your way," the gambler said quietly. He produced a pack of cards and squared them on the table. "Help yourself. Highest wins. Sudden death."

"You said it," the half-breed assented.

The fingers of his left hand closed over the cards, gripping them gently. A touch told him they had been prepared—the ends and sides of some of them treated with a file, so that the man who knew what had been done could cut high or low as he desired. He knew now why Baudry had given in, but it made no difference to his plan. He hesitated only for an instant and then lifted the whole pack and hurled it in the other man's face.

"Cold deck me, would you?" he cried, and snatching out his gun sent two bullets into the gambler's breast.

Grimacing horribly, hands reaching blindly for support, the stricken man collapsed like a house of cards. Navajo's smile was that of a demon.

"Sudden death it was," he said hoarsely, and turned to the girl, only to find her unconscious upon the floor.

Stuffing the roll of money into a pocket, the half-breed stood gloating over his captive for a moment or two, his lewd eyes dwelling on the graceful curve of her neck and the rounded white shoulder which Baudry's brutality had left exposed.

"A pretty piece—and mine—now," he exulted. "Well, beautiful, we'll be on our way."

Lifting the limp form, he carried it to where the gambler's horse was hitched outside the hut, and roped it to the saddle. He was about to mount his own beast when he remembered something; both the dead men would have money. He went back and was kneeling by the side of Baudry when a word rang out like a pistol shot.

"Navajo!"

Jim was standing in the doorway, a gun leveled from the hip. The icy, passionless voice fell on the outlaw's ears like a death knell. Though he had bragged to Baudry, he feared this cold-eyed young cowboy who had so quickly gained a reputation as a gunman. "Sudden death!" The phrase recurred to him with a new and ominous significance. Bitterly he cursed himself for his delayed departure; but for his greed . . .

Navajo rose slowly to his feet, his devious mind searching for a way out.

"These *hombres* appear to have bumped each other off," he said. "I was just seein' if they was cashed."

Still keeping the man covered, Sudden picked up Rogue's gun; it was fully loaded; the butt of Baudry's weapon could be seen protruding from its shoulder holster. He looked at the half-breed.

"Rogue reloaded and Baudry put his gun back after they was killed," he said sarcastically.

"I was guessin'—only bin here a few minutes and found 'em like this," the man replied sullenly.

"So it wasn't you who carried Miss Eden out?"

"Yeah, I was meanin' to take her back."

"Tied to the saddle?"

"Couldn't do no other way—she'd fainted."

"And the herd money. Takin' that back too?"

"Dunno nothin' about it."

Sudden laughed scornfully. "Yore a poor liar, Navajo," he said. "Hand over your gun."

Navajo stiffened. He remembered now that he had fired twice and had not replaced the charges. An examination of the weapon would produce apparently conclusive evidence and . . . During the conversation he had been edging backward an inch at a time. Now, with a quick sweep of one arm, he knocked the candle from the table and dropped prone to escape the expected bullet. None came, only a taunting voice:

"Fine! Figured you'd play it that way when I saw you sneakin' back. Don't waste no shots, Navajo; you only got four."

Jim was surmising, but correctly, and the outlaw gritted his teeth at the remainder. He must be sure, and now could he be in that blinding blackness? For there was no light; even the tiny unglazed window could hardly be located, so dark was the night outside. Flat on his belly the half-breed lay motionless, waiting for some movement which might betray his enemy's whereabouts.

An idea came to him—Baudry's gun. If he could obtain that and fire four shots, Jim would deem him defenceless, and . . . .He knew the direction in which the body lay and began to make his way toward it. Hardly daring to breathe, he crawled on inch by inch, feeling cautiously for obstacles. At length his groping fingers touched a still face, traveled downward and found a shoulder holster—empty. He stifled the curse which rose to his lips, and edged away.

"You ain't a quick thinker, Navajo," the taunting voice said. "I've got Baudry's gun."

In his rage and disappointment the half-breed fired at the spot where he judged the speaker to be. An answering spit of flame stabbed the gloom and a bullet nicked his neck. The voice spoke again:

"Near thing, Navajo. A mite to the right and you'd be travelin' the one-way trail."

The incident shook the outlaw's confidence. Hell! if the fellow could see in the dark. . . . And he had wasted a shot, for though the silence was profound again he knew that he had missed. Lying there in the stillness to pregnant with danger, he flogged his faculties to find a device to extricate himself and, at length, hit on a plan. It would be a desperate risk but he resolved to take it. And he must act at once, for he knew that his courage was ebbing; the jeering devil waiting so patiently to kill him was his master. Rising swiftly to his knees, he fired and swayed away instantly. Jim aimed at the flash, heard the thud of a falling body, and a deep groan. Five—ten minutes passed and no sound came. The cowboy moved a foot noisily but nothing happened.

Looks like I may've got him," he muttered.

Groping on the floor, he found the candle and lighted it. Navajo was lying on his side, his face buried in the bend of his left arm, his right arm hidden under his body. His gun lay some feet away. In the uncertain light he appeared to be dead. Sheathing his pistol, Sudden stopped to turn the body over. Instantly it came to life, the right hand darting upward in a vicious stab. With a lightning snatch the cowboy clutched the wrist, wrenched it aside, and springing back, pulled and fired. Navajo, his face ferociously distorted in a murderous grin, sank back. This time there was no doubt.

Chilled to the bone by the narrowness of his escape, Jim leaned against the wall. Had he delayed an instant, or missed the deadly thrusting wrist, eight inches of steel would have ripped him open. He drew a long breath, and wiped the cool moisture from his forehead. Then he looked at the dead man with an odd respect.

"Didn't figure you had the savvy for a play like that," he mused.

He searched for and secured the stolen money, and then the sound of a galloping horse straightened him up, gun in hand. It was Sandy who thrust open the door.

"Jim, you all right?" he called.

"Yeah, and I'm lucky," Jim reproved.

"Where's Carol?" the boy asked.

"Outside—tied to a hoss," Jim told him, adding grimly, "I've been too busy to turn her loose."

As they bent over Rogue, his eyelids flickered and his

lips breathed a question.

"She's safe," Jim assured him.

Sandy went out and found that Carol was conscious again. He untied and lifted her down. She asked about Rogue.

"He's badly hurt," the boy told her.

"I must go to him," she said.

"It's—pretty terrible—in there," he demurred.

"It would have been more terrible—for me—if he hadn't come," she cried, and to that Sandy could say nothing.

A spark of life shone in the dying outlaw's tired eyes when she entered the cabin. Kneeling by his side she strove to thank him, sobs choking her.

"It don't matter," he said.

"Can't I do anything?" she asked hopelessly.

A little shake of the head, and then, doubtfully. "Once I had a lass who would be about yore age. . . ."

With swift comprehension, she bent over and pressed her lips to the furrowed brow of the man who had killed and robbed, yet given his life for her.

"It's too good—an end—for a—rogue," he murmured.

The ghost of a smile passed over his hard mouth and that was all. Sandy led the weeping girl out of the hut, clumsily trying to comfort.

Through the black velvet of the night they rode back to town. Jim led the way, his thoughts dwelling on the dead outlaw. Though his meeting with the man had meant nothing but misfortune, he had liked him, and in some way he could not understand, was conscious of a sense of loss. The pair behind were riding close together, and Sudden smiled a little bitterly at the reflection that he was soon to lose another friend. Had Rogue lived. . . .

It was not until the morning that the rancher was sufficiently recovered to hear the full story of the previous night's happenings.

"By heaven, Jim, all the herd money wouldn't pay what I owe you," he said. "But you'll be comin' back to the S-E with me, an'—"

A shake of the head interrupted him. "I'm obliged," the cowboy replied, "but yore memory ain't workin'."

"Shucks! I got friends who can pull ropes," Eden said.

Jim's grin was sardonic. "I got enemies who can do the same and mebbe my neck would be in a loop of one," he pointed out. "No, I'm shore fond of Texas but I ain't intendin' to end my days there—yet."

Eden's gaze went to Sandy. "I'm told you kept them rats from finishin' me off," he went on. "You must have had a change of heart since the Colorado."

"Hold yore horses, and take a squint at these," Jim interposed, producing a pair of beaded moccasins. "Found 'em in Navajo's saddle bag; they fit those tracks I measured. And there's this."

The rancher took the proffered slip of paper. "Baudry's fist and signature," he muttered, and read the contents aloud: *"'I have today bet Navajo one thousand dollars that my friend, Sam Eden, gets his herd through and comes safely back to the S-E.'"*

The document bore the date the drive started. With knitted brows Eden studied it. "Why, he's offerin' the fella thousand cold to put me outa business," he burst out.

"You said it," Sudden agreed. "And when he failed to turn the trick hisself he bribed Lasker."

The old man looked at Sandy. "That appears to let you out," he said. "Suppose I'll have to take your word."

This ungenerous surrender brought a reproachful "Daddy!" from his daughter, and an expression of angry scorn on the young man's face.

"I ain't offern' it," he retorted. "Think what you please."

Aunt Judy flung herself into the discussion with her

usual impetuosity. "Sam Eden," she said sharply, "if I was your daugher—even by adoption—I'd box your stubborn ears." She slanted a bony finger at Sandy. "Do I have to tell you who that boy is?"

A slow smile softened the rancher's face. "No, that's my scamp of a son, Andrew Eden," he replied, and the harshness was gone from his voice also. "I figured he had you fooled, Judy."

The lady snorted. "Take more'n dyed hair and a wisp o' bunch grass on an upper lip to fool the woman he used to plague to death with his pranks," she retorted. "I knowed him right away, but I was curious."

"Your son, and you treated him so—unkindly?" Carol cried. "You could even think . . ."

The rancher wriggled uneasily and then shook his head. "Don't reckon I ever really believed that, but I had to be sure," he excused. "An' I wanted to see if he would stand the iron. I didn't know the game but I was willin' to play it his way, so I told Jeff an' Peg-leg to keep their traps closed— they savvied him too. How you come to be with Rogue, boy?"

"Got word he was rustlin' your cattle," Sandy explained. " later, I learned it was more serious and when he sent Jim and myself to join your outfit it looked like a chance to put a crimp in his plans."

"Why pretend to be a stranger?" Eden asked.

Sandy looked embarrassed. "You ain't rememberin' how we parted," he said.

"I've not forgotten," he admitted. "Threatened to fill you with buckshot if you showed up again, didn't I? Well, that's all past and done—I reckon we've both learned sense since that day. You've made good and I'm proud of you, son." His eyes twinkled as he went on, "It's a pity Carol don't like redheads—claims she's had enough trouble with me, but mebbe she—" He looked around the room and seemed surprised to find the girl had slipped away. "Now where in mischief has she gone? You better go find her, boy; somebody is liable to steal her again."

Sandy's old impudent smile was back. "Somebody's goin' to," he promised.

PRIME TIME **LB499-2 $1.95**
James Kearney **Novel**

The book that picks up where *Network* left off . . . The explosive novel of violent power struggles inside a giant television network. The United Television Network. Outside an austere glass facade . . . inside a seething hot bed of ambitious men and women whose motto was "show your rivals no mercy" . . . men and women who would get what they wanted at any cost. (Foil cover)

FLAME IN A HIGH WIND **LB500-X $1.50**
Jacqueline Kidd **Adventure**

A Powerful novel of romance and adventure on the high seas. The War of 1812 ended for all but Capt. Denny Poynter. Branded pirate, pursued by British and Americans alike, he fought and plundered his way around the world. But his reckless freedom would be soon jeopardized as his first lady, the sea, gave way to the fiery Renee.

THAT COLLISION WOMAN **LB501-8 $1.95**
Deidre Stiles **Novel**

Fleur Collison was known as the most beautiful and wilful woman in all England. The young Englishwoman would return to her ancestral home of Ravensweir despite the fact that it was inhabited by her former lover, now brother-in-law. She was determined to take what she wanted from the world . . . and her sister.

ELENA **LB502-6 $1.50**
Emily Francis **Mystery**

The commune on this small Greek island lived a placid life among ancient monuments and clear blue sea until Elena came. They gave her friendship and love. She brought them death.

HOW TO DIVORCE YOUR WIFE — **LB503-4 $1.95**
Forden Athearn — **Nonfiction**

Practical advice for men from an experienced divorce lawyer, Forden Athearn on what to do before you tell your wife, how to tell your wife, family, boss, how to select a lawyer, and more!

DAY OF THE COMANCHEROS — **LB504-2 $1.50**
Steven C. Lawrence — **Western**

Slattery had witnessed the rape, murder, and pillage by the savage Comancheros but it wasn't personal until they put him on the end of a rope. No one dared stop them. Someone had to.

KILLER SEE, KILLER DO — **LB505-0 $1.50**
Jonathan Wolfe — **Mystery**

It started out as an innocent Halloween party. But innocent soon turned to bizarre when the treats stopped and a trick involving voodoo brought death to the scene. Someone was jailed and Indian detective Ben Club meant to set him free.

GUNSMOKE — **LB506-9 $1.50**
Wade Hamilton — **Western**

Ben Corcoran had become boss of Sageville range by killing anyone who tried to settle. When the quiet gambler came to town no one took notice . . . until he led the farmers in bloody revolt. First Time in Paperback.

A PASSION FOR HONOR — **LB467KK $1.75**
Louise MacKendrick — **Nonfiction**

Jackson Devereaux had nothing but his rifle and a powerful sense of mission when he came out of the Everglades determined never to return. They called him "swamp-trotter" and other names—but never to his face. Because to insult him was to ask for sudden death. "King Jack" built his private kingdom, sired sons and daughters, but that was only the beginning. For when a man is king there are those who seek to topple him from his throne.

PLEASURE IS OUR BUSINESS — **LB468KK $1.75**
Jack Sandberg — **Nonfiction**

This is an explosive exposé of America's fastest growing, profit-making industry, the *total* relaxation center. Sandberg investigates Manhattan's expensive sex clubs . . . establishments that cater to the needs of the "establishment" . . . bars, restaurants, music, topless and bottomless young women in a variety of decors from the decadence of the Roman Empire to the pageantry and pomp of the Indian mosque. Whether cash or charge, anything could be had for a price.

BLOODY GRASS — **LB469DK $1.50**
Hobe Gilmore — **Western**

The U.S. Cavalry was busy with booze, squaws, and officers' wives. But Redband, the crazed renegade Sioux was on the warpath and would stop at nothing to have revenge on white men . . . and white women.

TARK AND THE GOLDEN TIDE LB470DK $1.50
Colum MacConnell **Fantasy**

Usurped heir to the throne of the Tumbling Cliffs, Tark and his mentor Morned the Flea journey from the town of Sorne to the Silver Mountains transporting the coveted blue sapphire that is the fabled gem of luck for the Sornese. This is Tark's journey: past the beasts of the Burning Wood, the pirates of the Shallow Sea, and the Princess of the Silver Mountains. But there, at journey's end he must mount his giant fighting camel and meet his deadliest foe—the usurper Akor-Lut, Warmaster of the Golden Tide.

BLOOD MONEY LB471DK $1.50
Aaron Fletcher **Western**

Bounty hunter Jake Coulter is back as he scours the west for outlaws with a price on their heads. Now they would know how it felt to be a hunted animal.

THE WICKED WYNSLEYS LB472DK $1.50
Alanna Knight **Gothic**

Mab Wynsley and her young actor fiancé buy a mansion as their future home. Until the marriage she would live there accompanied by her sister . . . but soon the house of hope is smashed and she finds herself, her sister, and her future husband actors on a stage of death.

Cherry Delight
THE DEVIL TO PAY LB473DK $1.50
Glen Chase **Adventure**

Cherry Delight is sent to France to investigate a cult of devil worshippers—extortionists who murder, rape, and maim for pleasure and profit. The Devil presided over the Black Mass and orgies. But he and his disciples were in for a surprise . . . they had never seen hell until Cherry arrived.

THE LIFE OF KIT CARSON **LB474ZK** **$1.25**
John S.C. Abbott **Golden West Series**

Christopher "Kit" Carson was a legend to his countrymen. Trapper, trailblazer, scout, and Indian fighter, Kit Carson would become part of American history at its most exciting time—the pioneering of the wild west.

THE YOKE AND THE STAR **LB475TK** **$1.95**
Tana de Gamez **Novel**

"This tense, compassionate novel has an animal warmth and female ferocity that is very moving indeed."

—*Kirkus Review*

"Expert story-telling, excitement and suspense."

—*Publishers Weekly*

Cuba was ready to explode into bloody revolution. Hannan, the American newsman, could feel the tension in the air, in the eyes of the people in the streets and cafes. Everybody was taking sides; there could be no neutrals in the coming conflict. Hannan thought he could stay out of it. He was wrong. Love for a beautiful revolutionary pushed him past the point of no return.

THE RETURN OF JACK THE RIPPER **LB476KK** **$1.75**
Mark Andrews **Novel**

An English acting company opened a Broadway play based on the bloody Ripper murders of 1888. Just as the previews began, a prostitute was found dead in a theatre alley—disembowelled, her throat slashed. Other murders followed, and soon the city was gripped in terror. Had the most monstrous figure in the annals of crime returned to kill again?

THE RED DANIEL **LB477DK $1.50**
Duncan MacNeil **Adventure**

The Royal Strathspey's, Britain's finest regiment, are dispatched to South Africa to take command in the bloody Boer War and find the most fabulous diamond in all of South Africa—The Red Daniel.

SLAVE SHIP **LB478KK $1.75**
Harold Calin **Adventure**

This is the story of Gideon Flood, a young romantic who sets sails on a slave ship for a trip that would change his life. He witnesses the cruelty of African chieftains who sell their own for profit, the callousness of the captains who throw the weak overboard, and his own demise as he uses an African slave and then sells her.

A SPRING OF LOVE **LB479KK $1.50**
Celia Dale **Novel**

"A fascinating story."

—*The Washington Star*

"An immaculate performance . . . unsettling, and quite touching."

—*Kirkus Review*

This sweeping novel chronicles a determined young woman's search for enduring love. No matter where it took her, she followed her heart. The man with whom she linked her fortunes was said to be dangerous, but she knew there could be no one else.

TIME IS THE SIMPLEST THING **LB480DK $1.50**
Clifford D. Simak **Science Fiction**

Millions of light years from Earth, the Telepathic Explorer found his mind possessed by an alien creature. Blaine was a man capable of projecting his mind millions of years into time and space. But that awesome alien penetrated his brain, and Blaine turned against the world . . . and himself.